# Overdue

**The Village Library Mysteries, Volume 2**

Elizabeth Spann Craig

Published by Elizabeth Spann Craig, 2019.

This is a work of fiction. Similarities to real people, places, or events are entirely coincidental.

OVERDUE

**First edition. November 19, 2019.**

ISBN: 978-1946227539

Written by Elizabeth Spann Craig.

# Chapter One

It was my break at the library and I was spending it in the most relaxing way I knew how: curled up in the lounge with our library cat, Fitz. Even better, I was reading one of my favorite 'comfort reads', *September* by Rosamunde Pilcher.

I was so sure I was going to have a relaxing break, I set a timer for myself on my phone to make absolutely certain I didn't leave the lounge late. When my timer went off, I was completely surprised that twenty minutes had passed.

I reluctantly pulled Fitz off of me and he curled up in the warm spot where I'd been sitting, still purring faintly in his sleep. He was a beautiful, laid-back, orange and white cat who loved nothing better than quiet times and curling up in laps. This is what made him, quite possibly, the best library cat in the world.

I walked back out toward the circulation desk before being intercepted by my boss, Wilson. Wilson was *not* laid-back. This is what made him, quite possibly, the best library director in the world.

Wilson, in one of his ceaseless suits, blurted, "We have a library trustee in the building. There's mention of lugging books around." He was experimenting with a very regimental-looking mustache that appeared nearly as stiff and bristly as he was. He rubbed it absently.

Wilson was always cognizant of what library board members were doing at all times. He was especially intuitive if he felt they needed any assistance. I was often recruited to help them out, although I'd found in the past they frequently weren't as excited about getting help as Wilson thought they might be.

"Is this for the Friends of the Library book sale?" I asked. "If they want to move some of the books for the sale upstairs from the basement, I can definitely give them a hand."

"Would you?" asked Wilson, relieved. "I'd do it myself but I have a meeting that I need to get to. Carmen is the trustee. Thank you."

I frowned. "Wasn't Tanya James supposed to be helping Carmen today?"

"Apparently, she hasn't shown up. That's why Carmen needs help," he said in a clipped tone. He glanced at his oversized watch, looked alarmed, and hurried away. "I've got to go."

Wilson was starting to remind me of the White Rabbit from *Alice in Wonderland*. I set out dutifully toward the door leading to the library basement. Of all our board members, Carmen was my least favorite. I did appreciate her organizational skills, her ability to get things done, and the way she was able to motivate people to do what she wanted them to do. But her sometimes condescending attitude and the way she'd interrupt when you were trying to speak with her made her difficult to work with. I suspected she'd frequently, if not always, gotten her own way. Carmen was a beautiful woman with piercing blue eyes brimming with intelligence, porcelain skin and long, blonde hair.

I strode toward the front entrance of the library, which had a door that led down to an old cellar that housed holiday decorations, old microfiche reels, and donated books for the Friends of the Library fundraising sales. The stairs were steep and not especially well-lit, so I left the door leading down to the basement open. I frowned as I saw a book on one of the top steps. Carmen must have dropped it. But Carmen seemed the type to pick up a dropped item immediately.

"Carmen?" I called down. "It's Ann. May I give you a hand with the books?"

There was no answer. And the basement, although rather roomy, certainly wasn't big enough where you could move out of earshot. "Carmen?" I asked again, my voice sharper.

I hesitated and then walked down the stairs, grasping the wooden rail as I went. I called her name again and stopped cold as I saw a figure crumpled at the bottom of the staircase, blonde hair covered with blood. Feeling strangely detached, I noticed there was a gash on the back of her head, though she'd fallen forward on her front.

As I stared, frozen in shock, a cheery voice from the doorway above called to me. "Ann? Wilson told me to ask if you needed a hand with the books."

It was Luna, my purple-haired coworker. She reached for the dropped book on the staircase, frowning. Then I stepped to the side to turn and she saw Carmen's body and gasped.

"I'll call an ambulance!" she said, pulling her phone out of her pocket.

I crouched by Carmen's body, carefully laying a hand on her neck and feeling for a pulse that wasn't there. I looked back up the stairs somberly. "Luna, she's dead."

# Chapter Two

A few minutes later, there was a flurry of activity at the library. Luna and I were sitting in the breakroom, drinking strong coffee and being attended to by Wilson, who'd quickly returned from his meeting. Fitz jumped into my lap and was quiet and alert as if sensing something was wrong. Luna reached over every minute or so to rub Fitz and soothe herself. Emergency services sent everything they had to the library: fire trucks, ambulances, and the police, but ultimately there was nothing more to be done for poor Carmen.

After about twenty minutes, Burton Edison, the police chief for the small town of Whitby, joined Luna and me in the breakroom as Wilson stepped out to speak with the staff. Burton was a big middle-aged man with a kind smile. Somehow, his mere presence served to calm me down. He greeted us solemnly and said, "How are you both holding up?"

I glanced at Luna, who seemed to have gotten some of her color back.

Luna said, "Better now." She gave a shaky chuckle. "But then, this coffee is strong enough to eat with a fork."

Burton smiled at her, his eyes crinkling at the corners. "I'm glad you're better. That must have been quite a horrible shock."

"Especially for Ann," said Luna, gesturing at me. "She's the one who really found Carmen. I was just there at the tail-end of the discovery." She gave a croaking laugh. "At first, I didn't even notice because I was distracted by a book Carmen dropped on the stairs. I love reading about those free solo climber guys and all I was thinking was I wanted to get to the book sale first so I could buy it. It was a signed copy even, made out to one of the trustees. Then I saw Carmen."

Burton asked, "What's your interpretation of what happened?"

Luna said, "Well, she fell down the stairs, didn't she? I mean, that's how it *looked*, anyway. Those steps are so steep and poorly-lit that it's a wonder nobody's pitched down them before." She paused and knit her brows. "She *did* just fall down the stairs, didn't she?"

Burton looked at me with his steady, thoughtful gaze. As if he *knew* the answer to Luna's question, but wanted to hear what I had to say. "What was your impression of what happened, Ann?"

I blew out a sigh, thinking back. "At first, that's what I thought. Luna's right—the stairs are a problem. We really need to add more lighting down there, but it's just such an old building, the electrical wiring here is complicated. Now, of course, after this? Wilson will have the stairs and basement outfitted with all sorts of safety equipment. He's probably out there making phone calls right now to line that work up. There was one thing I had a question about, though. When I was checking to see if she was all right, I got the impression she didn't *look* as though she'd simply fallen down the stairs."

Fitz looked intently at me with his intelligent green eyes as if hanging on my every word.

"You think she was pushed?" asked Luna, eyes huge as she looked incredulously at me. "Why do you say that?"

I hesitated. "Maybe she wasn't pushed. Maybe she was struck over the head with something heavy and then tumbled down the stairs. There was some sort of a gash on the back of her head. I thought it was odd that it was on the back of her head when she fell on her front."

Burton nodded. "Thanks for that, Ann. We've got the state forensics team here to check for exactly that kind of information. Now, you both know I'm new to Whitby and I only knew Carmen as a very slight acquaintance. What can you two tell me about her? Is there any sort of background information I should have?"

Luna winced. "Sadly, that would involve speaking ill of the dead."

"I don't think she's listening," said Burton gently.

Luna took a deep breath. "I'm not sure anyone here at the library really liked Carmen. She was a real mess. She could be condescending as anything. And she always liked things done her way. She was spoiled in that respect. I'm not sure anybody ever told her no."

Burton said, "And Ann? Do you agree with that assessment?"

I said, "Well, I really *respected* Carmen. That's probably the one positive thing I can say about her. When Carmen wanted to get something done, she could move mountains and make it happen. I've always felt very grateful she chose the library as her pet project because she managed to raise all sorts of money for us. Our programs have improved under her patronage. And we have more books and technology because of her enthusiasm and focus."

"But personally?" pressed Burton. "How did you feel about her personally."

I shrugged. "It wasn't really my place to have a personal opinion about her."

"Oh, come on," said Luna. She gave me a small shove. "You can't make me look like the only bad guy here."

"You're right; Carmen was a mess. Because she was so good at what she did, she discounted everyone else's attempts to help," I said.

"In what way?" asked Burton.

"She didn't work well in groups. I mean, at all. In many ways, she was a born leader and able to tell everyone else what to do. But when it came down to it, she was actually horrible at leading because she didn't trust anyone else to do as good a job as she did. Carmen was a perfectionist. So she'd take it all over herself," I said.

Luna said, "And of course it was always done ahead of time and perfectly."

"But Carmen would always be incredibly stressed out and irritable. She'd also be unjustly angry she'd had to do all of the work," I said. "After all, she'd been the one who'd left everyone deliberately out of the loop."

Burton said thoughtfully, "And how did the other folks feel? The ones who were *supposed* to be working on the fundraiser?"

Luna and I glanced at each other. "They were furious," we chorused.

I added, "Especially Tanya James. She is something of a control freak and it would drive her nuts that Carmen wouldn't include her. And I think it's fair to say the other folks felt the same way."

Burton nodded. "I can imagine that would be the case. So it sounds as if Carmen is really type-A, and difficult to work with."

"There was one other positive thing about Carmen." I felt the need to try to not seem as if I was somehow blaming the victim. "She was a good person to have on your side. A couple of weeks ago, I'd really dropped the ball at work and forgot to get the word out about a big library event. I felt terrible about it—the event had incredibly low turnout. I hadn't mentioned it in the library newsletter or on social media or anything. Somehow it completely slipped my mind. From what Wilson mentioned to me later, the board members had been really harsh about my mistake at their meeting. Carmen stood up for me and told them I was overworked and trying to juggle too much."

Luna looked at me with an inscrutable expression before looking down at her hands folded in her lap.

Burton nodded. "Is there anything else? Family, for instance?"

I frowned and looked back over at Luna. She shrugged. Finally, I said sheepishly, "Honestly, I don't think I ever asked her about her personal life at all. I'd have been afraid she'd snap at me. We always kept everything on a business basis."

"So when you were heading down into the basement a little while ago, she wouldn't have chit-chatted with you at all about your life or hers?" asked Burton. "If she had any upcoming plans with friends or that kind of thing?"

"Far from it. I'd have asked her how many books she wanted to move upstairs for the Friends of the Library book sale and where she wanted them to go," I said.

Luna said slowly, "I actually *do* know something about her family. I mean, I know you have someone to notify in town."

Burton leaned in a little as Luna was speaking uncharacteristically softly.

Luna said, "She has a brother here. I admit it, I'm nosy. And it's kind of boring to work a book fair with someone and not talk to them at all, so I asked her a bunch of questions. I'm sure Carmen was probably ready to run away from me by the end."

I smiled. "Luna, you can get anyone to talk. I'm sure Carmen would never have told me about her family if I'd asked. She'd probably have told me to mind my own business in no uncertain terms."

Luna smirked. "You just have to ask the right way, that's all. I hung on Carmen's every word and she liked that."

"She was the kind of person who liked being the center of attention?" asked Burton, still jotting down little notes.

Luna nodded. "She sure was. But we all like to be in the spotlight sometimes, don't we? Anyway, she has a brother here, but she didn't tell me his name. I just thought Burton should know there was family locally who needed to be contacted." She focused on Fitz, carefully scratching him under his chin as he purred loudly.

Burton made a note in his notebook. "Thanks. I'll check on that right after I'm done here. The last thing we need is for him to find out about his sister through village gossip."

He stood up and said, "I think this is enough for right now. Please let me know if there's anything else you think of. I'll give Wilson an update on everything. Naturally, the front entrance of the library is off-limits while the forensics guys are investigating, but you can leave by the back. I'm afraid we're going to need to close the library down for the rest of the day."

"I figured as much. I'll make signs to put on the doors." I walked over to a shelf that held supplies and pulled down a couple of sheets of printer paper and a Sharpie pen and quickly scrawled something out.

Luna said, "I can post the closing on social media, too." She paused. "Do you think you'll be able to find evidence here?"

Burton shook his head. "Unfortunately, we won't be able to really count on picking up much. Everyone in town has been here and there are hundreds of fingerprints and bits of DNA left behind. But we'll have to see if there's anything we can find out. We're also talking to everyone who's been in the library today to see if they saw or heard anything."

"Maybe someone saw something suspicious-looking," I said, giving Fitz a final stroke. "Just a heads-up, but I'm going to take Fitz home with me. I don't think it's a great idea for him to be here with the library full of police and the doors open all the time."

"Probably best not to tempt fate," agreed Burton.

Luna said, "That's all we need to make it an even more horrible day—if our library cat went missing."

I put a cat treat into Fitz's crate and he trotted happily in since he'd always had good experiences in the crate, going to my house where he was treated like a furry little king. Then I stood up with the cat carrier and my makeshift signs.

"Here, let me carry that for you," said Burton chivalrously and I handed him the carrier.

Luna and I walked out of the breakroom, into the library, and out the back door, passing all sorts of officers from the state police, the SBI, on the way out. Burton walked with us as a sort of escort, seeming to have something on the tip of his tongue to say, but never actually saying it. There were patrons being interviewed by officers, although not many of them since it had been an unusually quiet day so far.

I stuck the sign explaining the library closure on the back door and then handed the other sign to Burton to put on the front door behind the police tape. "Do you think a patron could even *get* to the front door of the library to see a sign?"

"Maybe if they arrive an hour or so before closing. I'll put the sign on the front door at some point," he said, taking it from me.

He strode over briefly to speak with Wilson and then walked back in our direction.

He turned as an officer called out to him. "I'll talk with you later," he said quickly to us. He set Fitz gently down on the pavement next to me.

Wilson was pacing near our cars and looked at us sympathetically. "Are you okay?" he asked us. "I came straight over from the meeting as soon as I heard."

"News traveled that fast?" I asked.

"One of the library techs texted me," he said. "Although I'm sure that news *is* traveling fast." And he made a face. If there's one thing Wilson worries about, it's bad publicity for the library.

"We're okay," I said, glancing over at Luna before confirming it was actually true. Luna had turned a sort of sickly white when she'd seen Carmen and I'd been worried that she was going to faint and possibly pitch down the stairs herself. I'd left Carmen, helped Luna to sit down, and called Burton.

Wilson said quietly, "Did they have any idea what happened? Was it some sort of accident? Why are the police shutting down the library?" He gave a fretful frown. "I knew I should have upgraded the lighting in that basement."

"It doesn't look like an accident," I said. "I think the police are investigating to find out. It looked to me like Carmen had sustained some sort of head injury before she fell down the stairs."

"Murder?" Wilson's voice hissed out. He gave furtive glances around to make sure there weren't any patrons around who could overhear. "I thought perhaps she took some sort of misstep on the stairs and simply fell. I know she ordinarily wears heels."

He was right about Carmen's footwear. She was inordinately fond of heels and I know if *I* wore those on the stairs, I would certainly have stumbled. But Carmen was a pro at wearing them

. . . she wouldn't have been clumsy on a staircase or anywhere else. "I'm afraid not. The police are closing us up for the day so they can look for evidence and speak with some of the patrons who were here and might have seen something."

Wilson said, "Who could have done such a thing? And how brazen of them to do it—right in public where anyone could have seen it happen. And at the *library*." His tone indicated this was the kind of sacrilege that would not be tolerated.

Luna said, "But it really *wasn't* that brazen if somebody was looking for an opportunity. After all, the library was quiet. Maybe they looked around to make sure no one was about to walk in or out and then hit Carmen over the head."

"How horrible," said Wilson, looking grim. "Well, I'm sure that with Burton on the case, he'll soon have some good leads." He paused. "I'll have to think of a distraction. Something to keep people from thinking about this crime when they think of the library. Something involving a certain orange and white cat."

He gestured to the cat carrier at my feet and Fitz started loud purring on cue. Wilson stooped and stuck a couple of fingers through the carrier. Fitz bumped lovingly up against them.

"Whatever you decide, just let me know," I said.

A truck barreled into the parking lot. The driver parked abruptly, thrust open his door and hopped out. A tall, tanned man with angry eyes and a tight expression marched toward the library entrance. He stopped, baffled, as he finally noticed the yellow police tape and the police cars. I recognized him as he turned around, peering in our direction. Blake Thompson. He and I had gone to high school together. What's more, he helped out at the library as a handyman from time to time.

"Blake? Can I help you?" asked Wilson in his professional library director voice. "I don't think we asked for any maintenance assistance for the building today, did we?"

"No, I was here for other reasons. What's going on?" asked Blake, running an agitated hand through his dark hair. He gave me a look of recognition. "Is the library closed or something?"

"Unfortunately so, at least for today. We're anticipating opening for our regular hours tomorrow," said Wilson.

Blake scowled at the library as if it had personally offended him. He spoke to Wilson again, "What's up? Gas leak or something?"

Wilson was always looking for a way to finesse a bad situation. There just really wasn't a way to finesse a murder that was sure to come out in the local paper the next day. He said in a tight voice, "The police are investigating a . . . death . . . on the premises. Standard procedure." He added quickly as if suspicious deaths happened at the library all the time.

Blake's expression went from aggravated to concerned. "A death? Somebody died at the library?"

He swung his head around and his gaze combed over the parking lot. It settled on what I knew to be Carmen's Mercedes convertible, which the police appeared to be carefully inspecting.

He paled. "Where's Carmen? She's here today. She told me she'd be here."

# Chapter Three

The three of us froze, realizing we were going to have to deliver some bad news.

Not immediately getting answers from us, Blake turned and strode a few steps toward the library.

Wilson gave me a pleading expression and I said, "Wait . . . um, Blake. It's blocked off. And . . . I have some bad news."

I took a deep breath and continued as Luna and Wilson gave me worried looks, "I'm so sorry to have to tell you this, but Carmen has passed away."

Blake swayed a little on his feet and I immediately opened my car door. "Please," I said, "take a seat. This must be a shock."

He plopped down into my front seat, staring blankly at me. "That can't be right. Are you sure?" he asked in a pleading voice.

I nodded my head. "I'm afraid so."

"But I just saw her! She was having lunch and she was absolutely fine." His eyes narrowed belligerently at me.

I glanced at Wilson and Luna but they didn't seem to be able to arrive at a better response than I could. I said carefully, "I'm very sorry. You must have been a good friend of hers."

Blake shook his head. "More than a friend." His voice was raw and he stopped talking for a few moments as he blinked rapidly to regain control. As he did, he watched the police in Carmen's car, removing evidence in plastic bags. He slumped in the seat. Realization that this was true washed over him and a look of horror washed over his face.

A couple of patrons approached carrying books and Wilson and Luna quickly stepped aside to speak with them, with some relief at escaping the uncomfortable conversation I was having. I continued standing by Blake.

In a few moments, he spoke gruffly. "Tell me what happened."

I did, leaving out anything that might sound too grisly and dwelling on the fact Carmen couldn't have suffered since she was nearly immediately discovered.

Blake listened, nodding his head from time to time and flinching others. Finally he slowly said, "I should have been here. I was near the library all morning long, driving past on my way to check the status at different work sites. I could have just dropped by."

"But you didn't know anything bad was going to happen. There was no *reason* for you to stop by," I said.

He shrugged. "Carmen told me she'd be hauling stuff around for the book sale. I could have given her a hand with them." His face darkened. "And I definitely could have stopped anybody who planned on doing her harm."

"You sound like a good friend to Carmen."

The word *friend* seemed to bother him again. He said, "We were more than friends, like I said. But yeah—we were two peas in a pod. I've never laughed with anyone the way I laughed with her."

Considering I rarely saw Carmen smile and certainly never saw her laugh, this seemed rather extraordinary to me. Also, I had a hard time seeing sophisticated Carmen in a relationship with Blake, although opposites did attract.

"And she definitely didn't just fall down the stairs?" he demanded.

I shook my head. "Not from what the police saw."

Blake glowered. "Then I know who did it."

I moved a little closer to him. "Who?"

Blake spat out, "Elliot Parker. Who else?"

The name rang a bell somewhere, but I couldn't immediately place him. "I'm sorry, I don't think I know him."

Blake said, "Elliot Parker. You work at the library? You probably know him. He's the kind of guy who reads all day long. He's gotta be in here constantly."

"He sounds familiar. I'm sure I'd probably know him if I saw him," I said.

He said darkly, "Anyway, Elliot's going to be in a ton of trouble, so I don't know if you're going to see him or not. I'm gonna tell the cops the first chance I get that I saw Elliot arguing with Carmen at lunch."

"At lunch *today*?" I asked.

"Today. Just a little while ago. And I know why they were arguing, too. Carmen told me yesterday she was going to break things off with Elliot. She was never serious with him, you see. She just liked having somebody to go to plays and concerts and stuff with. She was *dating* me. We were like two peas in a pod."

"Got it," I said.

Blake continued with a frown. "Although I don't get why Carmen would go out to lunch with a guy just to break up with him. Makes no sense at all to me. Why ruin a perfectly good lunch?"

I didn't say anything, which was fine because Blake kept talking. "Trust me, if she was killed, Elliot did it. Because that conversation they were having at lunch sure didn't look friendly. I was driving by, but almost pulled over because I could see how mad Elliot was. And Carmen didn't look happy, either. Elliot must have followed her back over to the library to keep arguing with her."

I said, "But would Carmen have gone into the library with him acting that way?" It didn't seem likely. Carmen wasn't the kind of person who liked to make a scene, and the library could be pretty quiet sometimes . . . like this morning.

Blake considered this. "You're right—she wouldn't have gone into the library with somebody on her heels yelling at her. So maybe Elliot was so mad that he decided to follow her in at a distance and give her that shove. Maybe he couldn't stand being thrown aside because Carmen wanted to exclusively date me instead of him."

I had the feeling that Blake had watched a lot of really dramatic TV shows. "Maybe so." I gave a noncommittal smile.

"I'm going to talk to one of the cops and tell them," he said grimly, getting up from the car and walking with great purpose toward the police tape. He was quickly intercepted by an officer and started talking to him, gesticulating as he did.

I glanced over at Luna, who was staring back at the library building.

"Hey, Luna, would you like me to drive you home?" I asked with concern. She really hadn't recovered from our finding Carmen earlier and was still pale.

Luna shook her head automatically and then stopped and looked at me.

Wilson said sternly, "Luna, if you're still feeling upset or in shock, you really shouldn't be driving. Either Ann or I will be happy to take you home."

"But then my car will be here. I never know if Mom needs me to run any errands or anything. And then there's work tomorrow to drive to," said Luna, holding her hands out.

I said, "Wilson could drive your car home while I'm driving you. Then I'll drive him over to the library to his own car. It's not like Whitby is a huge town or anything . . . it will take us all of five minutes."

Luna glanced over at Wilson, who nodded in agreement. She smiled at us. "That would be great then, thanks."

She handed Wilson her car keys and climbed into my passenger seat while I put Fitz, still purring loudly, in the back seat.

When I pulled up to Luna's driveway, she gloomily regarded the house where she and her mother lived. "I'm going to have to tell Mom about this with me being home early and everything. But I may downplay my part in it."

"You didn't *have* a part in it. You didn't even technically discover Carmen since I was there a little before you. She'll be fine. The important thing is, you're safe."

Luna flushed and for a moment I thought she was going to say something. She apparently reconsidered, squeezed my hand, and waved at Wilson, who'd just carefully pulled her car into the garage. "Thank you. You're a good friend."

Wilson climbed into my passenger seat as Luna let herself inside the small house. He buckled up and turned to look into the back of the car where Fitz lay contentedly in his cat carrier. Fitz purred when he saw Wilson looking at him.

Wilson relaxed a little at the interaction with Fitz. "What a day. I didn't have the chance to ask you if you had any idea who might have been that upset with Carmen."

I glanced over at him. "You mean *that* upset? No, I don't have a clue."

"No one you work with has seemed angry with her? Or expressed that they were angry with her?"

I frowned. "Are you trying to get at something? Do *you* know about someone at work who might have been upset with Carmen?"

He instantly brushed off the suggestion. "Of course not. I have great respect and admiration for the staff. They would never do something like this."

But somehow, I got the impression he was trying to convince himself.

"Fitz is key as a distraction," said Wilson. "I was thinking about this the whole time on the way over here."

I backed out of the driveway and headed back in the direction of the library and Wilson's car. "You know, people aren't going to start thinking of the library as a dangerous place. It was a single incident and Burton is on the case."

Wilson said, "Maybe. But we could still use a distraction from it all. I've been reading up on engagement methods libraries are using on their social media. A Q&A is one approach. We could ask patrons to throw any questions they want to at us and we could post answers later on."

"I think our librarians are handling that already, aren't they? I know I get a ton of questions every day, from people not sure how to use social media to people who are looking for help with their family trees," I said.

Wilson considered this for a moment. Then he snapped his fingers. "I've got it. Dear Abby."

I glanced away from the road for a second to give Wilson a bewildered look. "Sorry?"

"You know—the advice columnist."

I said slowly, trying to divine some sense from what he was saying, "So, you're wanting the library to start an advice column?"

He nodded rapidly. "That's right. Here, I'll email the idea to you so we won't forget. It's been a crazy enough day so that things might fall through the cracks."

I pulled into the library parking lot. "I might be a little slow today, but I'm not sure I totally *get* your idea."

Wilson, still typing on his phone, said absently, "The library is all about offering advice, isn't it?"

I thought about this. "Sometimes. It's usually more about offering information."

Wilson ignored this. "But sometimes people need advice for things that they are embarrassed asking about."

I nodded, pulling into a parking place. "This is true. I've helped people who needed to do research on medical problems and they definitely seemed uneasy about asking."

Wilson said, "There must be *tons* of things that patrons would like help with that they're hesitant about sharing. What if we allowed them to be anonymous about it and then shared the results publicly? They could write questions on slips of paper and put them in a box on the circulation desk. They could also email them to us and we'd say everything that came in would be treated confidentially. On whatever topic! We wouldn't have to answer all the entries, of course, just the most interesting ones or the ones that might be helpful to most people."

I was relieved to hear that we weren't going to try to address them all since I had a sinking feeling that this project could be *Ye Olde Time Suck*.

Wilson was really getting fired up now. He loved brainstorming ideas for library engagement. "And, instead of Dear Abby, it could be Dear Fitz! We could put a cute picture of the cat on the box and on the slips of paper that they write their questions on. And as a header on social media."

I could see where he was going with it, but I still had some questions. "But Dear Fitz makes it sound as if we're offering . . . or rather . . . the *cat* is offering relationship advice. Not just a Q&A type thing."

Fitz purred his approval from the backseat.

Wilson said, "That's exactly it. Like I said, Dear Abby. Oh, we *could* answer the odd academic question, for sure. But we could also open it up to advice for handling life. Or relationship advice."

"And who," I asked, trying to sound polite and deferential still, "will be the person behind Dear Fitz? Who will be answering the questions?"

Now Wilson was being a bit canny. I could tell that he wanted to put it all on my shoulders but that he thought I might be spread a little thin. It was good of him to realize this, since I'd already worked quite a bit of overtime this week.

"Well, I think you'd be an excellent person for the job, Ann. Of course, it wouldn't *just* be you. The staff could all pitch in and you could read us some of the submissions when we have our morning meetings."

I said, "You realize that I haven't had a successful relationship myself in ... well . . . *ever.*"

"But you're wise beyond your years, Ann. You'll be the perfect candidate to spearhead the project," said Wilson.

I could tell that he was beyond listening at this point and very excited about his idea. He climbed out of my car, barely sparing a worried glance at the police tape and the officers still milling around the grounds. "We'll work on it first thing tomorrow," he said brightly as he closed the door.

I drove home with Fitz, my mind still spinning and not with Wilson's advice column, either. I still was having a tough time wrapping my head around the idea that someone murdered Carmen. As tough and unpleasant as she could sometimes be, there was no getting around the fact that she had done a lot of good in the small town of Whitby. Maybe she hadn't gotten the appreciation she deserved because of her abrasive manner and the fact she was both wealthy and beautiful.

Absently, I parked the car in front of my cottage and pulled the cat carrier out of my backseat. I set it down as I tried to find the front door key and heard someone calling my name behind me.

# Chapter Four

I turned around and saw Grayson Phillips. As always, I made a little gasp I hoped was inaudible. He was someone I was romantically interested in, although he was dating a friend of mine and so off-limits. I always felt like anytime I was around Grayson, I was uncommonly clumsy and had a hard time speaking intelligently. I kept hoping I'd be cured of this malady, which made me feel like a 7th grader, but as yet I hadn't happened upon a cure.

Since he'd moved in down the street, I'd always enjoyed my conversations with him. He was a reader and I saw him regularly in the library, although not as regularly as I'd have liked. He usually had kind eyes and a twinkling smile, but I saw neither of those right now.

"Something wrong?" I asked, frowning in concern at him.

Something was definitely wrong. His eyes were red and his nose was, too.

He said, "I just spoke with the police chief thirty minutes ago."

My frown deepened. I knew Grayson had been dating my friend, but had he perhaps also been seeing Carmen? He certainly looked upset. "About Carmen King?"

He nodded and took a deep breath. "You probably didn't know. There was no *reason* for you to know and we didn't have the same last name."

They were married? Divorced?

"She's my sister. Was my sister," he said, in a grating voice.

I blinked at him, likely looking like a complete dolt. He and Carmen hadn't looked a thing alike, aside from both being good-looking. For a second, I was worried I'd said something aloud and I put a hand across my lips to keep any other inane utterances from finding their way out.

Apparently I hadn't spoken though because Grayson said, "You didn't know. Like I said, there was no reason for you to—we didn't look anything alike. Carmen looked more like Mom and I favored Dad."

Finally able to find my voice, I said, "I'm so sorry. You're right—I had no idea." I paused for a second and said, "But neither of you are from Whitby, is that right?" I was trying to figure out how two siblings ended up in the same small town with neither one of them being from around here.

He nodded, gaze a little absent. "That's right. I followed Carmen down here. I was in between jobs and hunting for another, and Carmen let me know about an opening on the paper here. I came down to find out more and ended up staying." He gave a heavy sigh. "Burton gave me the scoop on what happened this morning and my first instinct was to go right over to the library and see the scene for myself. But Burton very gently reminded me that it was a crime scene and that everything was blocked off."

I said, "Yes, they've closed the library for the rest of the day while they investigate."

Grayson said, "This hasn't become real to me yet so I'm trying to find out more. Burton said you were the one who found Carmen."

I took a deep breath. "I was. And I'm so sorry, again, that you're going through this. I had no idea that Carmen was your sister. Even though she spent a good deal of time at the library, we never talked about personal things."

He gave a crooked smile. "That was Carmen, always business-minded."

I said, "Wilson, our director, asked me if I could give Carmen a hand bringing books out of the basement for the Friends of the Library book sale. There were quite a few books down there and the library was quiet at the time. When I got to the door leading to the basement, it was open and the light was on, so I figured that Carmen was already downstairs. When she didn't answer me and I got a little closer, I found her."

Grayson asked quietly, "She was already dead?"

I quickly answered, "She was. And I'm not a medical expert, but for what it's worth, it must have been quick. There was no time for her to have suffered. Wilson asked me to help right after he'd spoken to Carmen and I stopped what I was doing to go directly there. What's amazing is that there was time for anyone to have . . . well, to have done what they'd done," I finished awkwardly.

Grayson nodded. "Thank you for that. I was worried somehow she'd been lying at the bottom of the basement stairs for a while and had been hurting." His voice cracked at the end.

We stood quietly for a few seconds, Grayson trying to regain control of his emotions and me trying to figure out what I could possibly say. Finally, I realized that I hadn't even invited him in, I'd been so shocked at finding out that Carmen and he were sister and brother.

"Please, can you come inside?" I asked. "Sit down for a few minutes?"

He hesitated and then nodded. "Thanks."

I leaned over to pick up Fitz, but Grayson beat me to it. "Hey, little guy," he said gently as he moved the carrier inside. As soon as Grayson set down the carrier, he opened the latch and Fitz bounded out, bumping lovingly against him. Grayson stroked the cat and said, "Animals are amazing. I can actually feel my stress level decreasing as I'm petting him."

I smiled at him. "Fitz is becoming quite the comfort animal. I've never seen a cat that's so good with so many age groups and types of people. Can I get you something to drink? Or to eat?"

Grayson shook his head. "No, but thanks. My appetite has disappeared, for the time being, anyway."

"Maybe a water?" I asked. My great-aunt who raised me was always such a great hostess and I tried to live up to her legacy as much as I could.

"Actually, that would be great," he said. He took a seat on one of my cushy sofas, sinking into the surface as Fitz jumped up to join him.

I came back a few seconds later with a couple of tall glasses of water. He took one and drained half of it in a couple of gulps.

"Sorry." He laughed. "I guess I didn't realize how thirsty I was." He paused. "Ann, do you have any brothers or sisters?"

I shook my head. "I'm afraid not. I was an only child. I can't imagine what you must be going through."

Grayson said thoughtfully, "It's a funny thing with siblings. You can be amazingly different from your sister or your brother, even if you're genetically very close. Carmen and I could fight like cats and dogs, although we also always had each other's backs. I feel bad about the fighting now."

I thought back to Luna, feeling regret for her own squabble with Carmen. I said, "That's pretty typical sibling behavior though, from what I've always heard. You shouldn't worry about it."

Grayson sighed. "You're right, although this one was more than just a tiff. It's one of those things where I felt bad about it later. Most of the time when we argued, it was just because the two of us were so different and had different approaches to things. And Carmen always thought I was overprotective of her and gave me some push-back for that." There was a faint smile on his lips at the memory.

"Were you the older brother, then?" I asked.

He chuckled. "You'd think so, wouldn't you? But no, I was the baby brother. But still overprotective. This last argument, though, wasn't because I was trying to boss her around." He paused. "Sorry. I don't really have anybody that I can talk to about this stuff. Carmen and I had older parents and, sadly, they're both gone. I'd talk to my best friend about it, but my best friend is involved."

"I don't mind," I said quickly. "At the library, I've learned to be a good listener."

"I bet you have, considering how much time you spend with the public every day. It's just that Carmen was dating my best friend," said Grayson. He made a face. "Carmen's relationships never went very well."

"Unlucky in love?" I asked lightly.

"More than that. Tyrannical in love. It was always Carmen's way or the highway. I tried to warn Elliot, but he was too besotted to listen to me. He figured I was just being overprotective. I *was*, but not overprotective of Carmen, but of Elliot. Carmen wasn't the best person in the world to have a relationship with," said Grayson.

"You said 'tyrannical.' Was it that she wanted to spend a lot of time with her boyfriends?" I asked.

"Completely the opposite, actually. The poor guy would end up mooning around over her and she'd lose interest. That's when Carmen would find someone else to date," said Grayson, eyes dark.

"And she'd end the relationship to pursue another one?" I asked.

"Not even. She'd cheat on the first guy with the second one." Grayson's voice was stiff.

"So you think that she might have been seeing someone else at the same time she was seeing your friend?" I asked.

"I'm sure of it. I saw the two of them together. Later that day, I stopped by her house and let Carmen have it. She was outside planting flowers around her mailbox and I'm sure the whole neighborhood must have heard me. But I was mad on Elliot's behalf. He's just this quiet, gentle guy who never realized what he was getting himself into."

I frowned. "Elliot. He wouldn't be Elliot Parker, would he?"

Grayson lifted his eyebrows. "You know him?"

I said, "Not much, but I see him in the library quite a bit. He requests a good number of books and I'm the one who usually puts them in the reserved section with his name on them. He seems like a big reader."

Grayson nodded. "He's a professor over at Whitby College. He's not exactly the type of guy that I'd have pictured my sister with—he's quiet and intellectual and isn't crazy about going out to dinners or events. Usually, she chooses to go out with someone more extroverted. Plus, I sort of felt guilty about the fact I introduced them."

"You set them up?"

"Nothing like that. I was just having lunch with Elliot downtown when Carmen came in. She makes quite an impression when she wants to, and she decided she wanted to make the effort with Elliot. I think he was blown away," said Grayson, making a face.

"But you regretted it later?" I asked quietly.

"Exactly. My sister wasn't exactly the most loyal of girlfriends. I don't think I realized how much she strayed until I moved down here and saw for myself. I happened to notice she was making out with her handyman." Grayson's face reddened at the memory.

I winced. "That must have been upsetting."

"Well, it was upsetting for me, but I don't think it was upsetting for Carmen. She just rolled her eyes at me and told me to grow up. The guy she was with looked so confused, like he thought I was going to slug him or something. When he realized I was her brother, he *still* looked alarmed. I was pretty mad at the time."

"Where was this happening?" I asked.

He sighed. "That's the thing. It was outside the library. So not only was Carmen indiscreet, I wasn't being discreet either. When I launched into a rant, there were all kinds of people around. Burton actually mentioned the fact that Carmen and I argued when he spoke to me."

My eyes opened wide. "That's pretty quick intel even for a small town."

Grayson nodded. "Yeah. I'm just trying to get used to Whitby still." He took a sip of his water. After a moment he said, "I just can't seem to take it in. That someone could be angry enough at Carmen to do something like this to her. I mean, I know Carmen was difficult to deal with." He gave a short laugh. "*I* found Carmen difficult to deal with. But most of the time, Carmen just did these petty little things. Nothing to make someone want to murder her. It's crazy to even think about. Can you help me to try to make sense of this?"

His voice was pleading. I hesitated, feeling awkward. But he was looking at me so beseechingly. "I don't know, Grayson. Can you think if Carmen gave any clues lately to anything that might be bothering her? Was there anyone in particular she was having issues with? Anything like that?"

Grayson thought about this. "Carmen's relationships were always bumpy and most of the time it was Carmen's fault. She didn't really talk to me much about them. Although I did notice some tension between Carmen and her best friend recently. Carmen and I were out together and she quickly had us dodge into a shop to avoid her."

"Who was her friend?" I asked.

"Mel Trumbull. She hangs around the library some, so you might know her." He shook his head. "I have no idea what their tiff was about. But there was definitely something there. Mel has always been a great friend for Carmen—really loyal and kind. I have no idea what happened between them. But if I had to guess, it was something Carmen said or did." Grayson sighed. "She didn't mean it, but Carmen could be very abrasive." He looked over at me. "Did you ever have any issues with her? I'd be surprised if you didn't."

No. I'd never had any issues with Carmen because I always bit my tongue. She would make snide or cutting comments from time to time and I always pretended I didn't hear them or that they didn't bother me because I knew that it was important to my director that I got along with Carmen.

I said to Grayson, "I might have seen a little abrasiveness from her, but I never had any problems with your sister. Plus, she did something really kind for me recently and stood up for me in a meeting with other board members. I appreciated that. Plus, she was a great supporter of the library. We're really going to miss having her help there."

He nodded, looking pleased. "The library was always one of her pet projects. She loved reading and everything that the library represents—freedom of information, access to resources. She was just fortunate she was able to devote as much time and energy as she did to her volunteering and charity work."

I had to admit I'd always been a little curious about Carmen's independence. She wasn't employed, but never seemed short on funds, either. And she lived in a wonderful area of Whitby in a large, historic home. I just paused, hoping that Grayson would fill in the gaps without my having to ask.

Fortunately, he did. "We were lucky enough that our grandparents and parents provided for us financially after they passed so that we never really had to worry about finding a financially lucrative job. But Carmen took things a step further when she married an investment banker right out of college. Unfortunately, he soon died in a car accident."

"I'm sorry," I said, shaking my head. "He must have been very young."

Grayson shook his head with a wry smile. "Not as young as Carmen, no. She was his second wife. But again, she was left well-provided for. She was happy to leave New York and come down to Whitby."

"Why Whitby?" I asked. Then I shook my head. "Sorry. Just curious. We have such a small town that I'm always interested when folks find their way here."

Grayson said, "No worries. It was kind of an odd choice for someone like Carmen. We were actually familiar with the area because we'd come here to see our grandparents when we were kids every summer. It was the kind of place that represented peace and quiet and happy times to us. I guess that's what attracted Carmen. Then, when I was looking for a change of pace, it attracted me, too. Plus, I was able to stay at Carmen's house while I was looking for a place of my own. It just made everything easy."

I nodded and said hesitantly, "I get it. That's immediately what I felt when I moved here when I was a kid. It felt like a real community . . . and safe. Very peaceful."

Grayson took a final sip of his water and walked it into my kitchen to put the glass in my dishwasher. He leaned over to give Fitz a final rub. "Thanks for the water and for talking to me about all this. I feel a little better. You know how the cops are—they can only tell you so much."

I nodded and said, "Again, I'm really sorry about everything. Feel free to come by and talk anytime."

He walked out and I locked the door behind him, leaning against it. Carmen had been a complicated person with apparently a lot of complex relationships. I didn't envy Chief Edison at all as he tried to figure out what had happened to her.

Fitz, sensing my tension, hopped on the sofa and rolled on his back, turning his head to look coyly at me. I chuckled and sat on the sofa next to him. He was the first cat I'd ever seen who didn't mind a tummy rub. Most cats *seemed* to be inviting a tummy rub, but as soon as you tried one, they attacked your hand. Fitz loved tummy rubs. And, as Grayson had mentioned, my tension dropped away as I rubbed him.

I glanced across the room at the book I was *supposed* to be reading. One of my film club regulars, Timothy, really wanted me to read his favorite book. Every time film club met, he asked me excitedly if I'd read it and each time I had to admit defeat. I hated doing that because Timothy was such a cool kid—he was high school age and wanted to share his favorite book with me. Now I was determined to make some progress . . . except the book was James Joyce's *Ulysses*. At close to seven hundred pages, I'd barely made a dent in it. And it wasn't what I'd call a comfort read, not after the day that I'd had so far.

So I pulled *September* back out of my work backpack. Fitz and I curled up with each other and I spent the rest of the day reading.

# Chapter Five

T he next morning, Wilson called me early.

"The police are allowing us to open to the public," he said, relief evident in his voice. "They must have gotten everything they needed yesterday. Although the basement will still be sealed off, of course."

"That's good," I said. "I'll pack Fitz up and we'll be right there."

"Yes, be sure to have Fitz back there. You'll work on the advice column when you get in, then?"

Wilson was clearly totally enamored with his idea. It made me smile.

"I'll be sure to make it a priority," I promised. I knew what this assignment was going to mean—me doing plenty of research to ensure "Fitz" gave appropriate advice and included good references and resources for people who needed further help.

Fitz walked right into his carrier again and we headed back to the library. Sure enough, the police tape had been removed and the police cars were gone. I unlocked the back door and stepped inside, carefully letting Fitz out. He purred and bumped against me and then went prancing off into the stacks.

I walked around, turning on lights and straightening chairs. Because we'd left so abruptly, there were also books and magazines to shelve.

I heard the door open and turned around to see Luna coming in. She was looking much more like her unflappable, laid-back self. Although instead of her usual brightly-mismatched clothing she was looking more subdued today, wearing an ensemble of all-black, including a pair of black, high-topped shoes that added a bit of spunk to an unusually-grim outfit.

"Hey, thanks again for taking me home last night." There was just a glimpse of the Luna from yesterday. Then she briskly added, "I'm much better today. Guess I don't take to unpleasant surprises anymore. Plus, I don't handle death well. Good thing I never wanted to go into the medical profession."

I smiled at her. "Glad you're better. Were you able to get some sleep?"

Luna nodded. "Yes. And I ended up talking to my mom about it since she was bound to find out from somebody. Actually, it ended up being a good thing because she talked me completely out yesterday. Whew! We examined Carmen's death from every angle possible."

"And that helped?" If I'd talked it out to that extent, my head might be spinning too much to go to sleep. I walked to the circulation desk and Luna followed, slouching against it.

"I guess talking it through was what I needed to do," said Luna with a shrug. "I wasn't processing it otherwise."

"I'm glad she was such a big help. How's your mom doing?"

Luna brightened. "She seems to be doing better lately. Not as many aches and pains and she's been more interested in leaving the house. I'll bring her by here soon. Now if only our money worries would turn around as fast as Mom's health issues! I made a resolution to pack my lunch every day. No more trips to the vegan deli for me."

I said ruefully, "I should follow your lead."

"You pack your lunch almost every day!"

"The key word there is *almost*. The problem is that some days I come home and just don't feel like cooking or haven't planned what I'm going to eat. Or if I *have* planned it, I haven't picked up all the ingredients at the store. On those nights, I snack at home and then the next day I don't have leftovers to bring. And I frequently don't have sandwich stuff because I ate them for supper. I guess I just have to be more organized at the beginning of the week to plan a menu and then go to the store to pick up everything." As usual, I was already starting to follow this rabbit hole of thought instead of focusing on what I was supposed to be—which was setting up an advice column for Fitz.

Luna drummed her fingers on the table in an unusual nervous gesture. My gaze was drawn by the clicking of her long fingernails, coated in a rich black nail polish. I blinked. "Wow, your nails have really grown out."

She snorted. "Nope. I bit them all off last night from nerves. These are acrylics. Putting these on last night was a good distraction from what had happened."

I looked down ruefully at my own stubby, sensible nails. "I ought to follow your example, yet again."

"Oh, your nails are fine—they suit you. They're practical, just like you are. Anyway, like I was saying, the acrylics were something to get my mind off things. I tell you, Ann, I was really shaken up. The library seems like a haven to me, you know? A harbor in the storm. I was surprised how much Carmen's death bothered me. I mean, you had to drive me home!"

I said, "I think we all have different reactions to deaths. Besides, that was a really abrupt tragedy and Carmen was a young woman. Of course it was upsetting."

Luna glanced toward the door and raised her eyebrows. "You don't have a new admirer, do you?"

"*New* admirer? I don't even have an old one," I said.

Luna said, "Well, there's a man coming through the door with flowers and we're the only women in here. And I'm not dating anyone."

I followed her gaze and saw a man in his 30s carrying a bouquet of flowers. His glasses gave him a studious look and he was attractive with dark hair flopping on his forehead that he impatiently pushed back. He was also in a suit, minus the jacket. I recognized him as Elliot Parker.

"He's one of our patrons," I said slowly. "In fact, I think he may possibly be someone who was dating Carmen."

Luna's eyebrows flew up. "How did you discover that little tidbit? Carmen didn't seem like the type to be engaging in a library romance."

"She wasn't. I think she was a very private person. But Blake told me about it." I paused. "There's something else. When I was back home yesterday, I ran into Grayson. *He's* Carmen's brother. The one whose name you didn't know yesterday."

"What?" Luna's eyes were huge. "You're joking. *Your* Grayson?"

"I don't have a Grayson." I sighed.

"Not yet. But the Grayson who lives on your street? And is dating that horrible woman?"

I snorted. "Thanks for being supportive, but she's not really a horrible woman. You know Trista is a friend of mine. And yes, that very same Grayson. Not that there are many of them around."

"Wow. I mean, I can hardly even believe it. Those two are *nothing* alike. Grayson, when he's been in the library, anyway, seems so friendly and outgoing. He actually smiles. I can probably count on one hand the number of times I saw Carmen smile and they were all at official library events. She had one of those really tight, reluctant smiles, too, not like Grayson's wide grin. No, I'd never have guessed it. They don't look anything alike. And they didn't *act* anything alike, either."

Luna was right. Grayson was easygoing with a smile never far from his face. Carmen was uptight and you had to win her smiles just as you had to win her approval.

"Anyway, he mentioned this patron who's coming in with the flowers. His name is Elliot. He's a friend of Grayson's and also dated Carmen," I said in a low voice.

"And he's heading this way," said Luna. She sighed. "Unfortunately, I've got to set up for storytime. Let me know what he says, okay? To be continued!" And she rushed off.

The man approached me hesitantly. "Hi, I'm Elliot Parker. I know I've seen you here many times."

I reached out my hand and shook his free hand. "I'm Ann Beckett, one of the librarians here. Is there anything that I can help you with?"

He nodded, again seeming very hesitant. "I don't usually do this. Well, fortunately, I don't ordinarily have a *reason* to have to do this. But I wanted to bring flowers to memorialize Carmen King. I'm sure you knew Carmen, working in the library as you do?"

I nodded. "I sure did. And I'm so sorry for your loss; it sounds as if you were a friend of hers. We have a vase in a storage room and I can put the flowers on a small table at the front of the library if you like."

He paused. "Was the front of the library near where she . . . passed?" he asked quietly.

"It is. Would that work?" I asked him.

He nodded again, a sad look in his eyes as he handed me the flowers. "It would. I'm sorry—I just can't believe that she's gone. I just had lunch with her yesterday."

A lunch, as I recall, that Blake said ended in an argument. I wondered if that had anything to do with the guilt and grief that I saw etched on Elliot's features.

Before I could repeat my condolences, Elliot frowned and asked, "Are you the librarian who found her? The police chief mentioned a member of the staff had discovered Carmen."

I nodded. "I was. I was on my way to give her a hand with the friends of the library book sale." I hesitated. "If it gives you any comfort at all, I don't think she could have suffered at all. I was there very quickly after it happened."

Elliot said, "So the police were telling me the truth. I wondered if they were just trying to be kind. They also told me she'd been unconscious before she fell. I just thought how horrifying it must have been for Carmen to pitch down the staircase." There was a catch in his voice as he spoke.

I said, "It sure sounds as if she didn't suffer at all." I paused. "Did you know Carmen long?"

Elliot gave a short laugh. "Was it possible for anyone to really *know* Carmen? How well did you know her?"

I shook my head. "I'm afraid that I only knew her on a professional level. We spoke sometimes, but only regarding projects at the library."

Elliot said, "I knew her a bit better than that, but I still feel as if she was a mystery to me in many ways. We were dating each other. I feel so terrible that I wasn't here. Maybe, if I'd been able to help her out with the book sale, none of this would have happened."

"Or perhaps whoever did this would simply have picked another time and place," I said softly. "You shouldn't feel guilty about this."

He continued absently, "I still should have been here. I didn't have a class yesterday afternoon. I could have helped out but I wanted to clear my head. I ended up going for a walk on one of the trails. I sometimes do that because it really helps me to sort things out. If I'd only known something like this was going to happen, I could have just helped out at the library instead. I'm here frequently anyway, as you know."

I nodded. He was probably a once-a-week patron at least. "I'm sorry. I'm sure the police will get to the bottom of whoever is responsible for this."

Elliot's voice turned sharp. "Maybe the police should be looking at her friends."

"Her friends?"

"She had one friend that she'd been arguing with lately." He sighed. "Carmen wasn't always the kindest of friends. On the one hand, she could be incredibly loyal. But on the other, she could be a bit of a backstabber. I think this particular friend, Mel, felt the backstabbing lately."

I pricked my ears up a little. Grayson had mentioned Mel, too.

Elliot continued, "The funny thing is Carmen could also be a fantastic friend. She remembered *everything*. I was surprised one time when Carmen showed up at my office with flowers and take-out for our one-month anniversary." He had a faint smile on his mouth at the memory. "I felt like we were kids again: like a one-month anniversary was actually reason to celebrate. We streamed some music and danced in my office until a student showed up for office hours."

I smiled at him. "It sounds as if you were both really close."

Elliot said, "It does sound that way. But then, on the other hand, she could be tough to deal with. Sometimes the same exact day. In fact, later on that anniversary, she called me up and complained about the fact that I hadn't texted her back an hour before."

I said, "She expected immediate responses from you?"

He nodded. "Immediate. And I'd been teaching a class. I don't have my phone on when I'm teaching—I don't like it when my students are on their phones when I'm trying to teach and I sure wouldn't want them to see *me* up there texting when I've asked them not to."

"Did it blow over? I mean, was she the kind of person who'd be upset for short periods of time and then she was fine a few minutes later?" I asked.

He shook his head. "No. She was one to nurse grudges. And when Carmen froze you out, you really *felt* frozen. It was like being separated from the sun."

I couldn't imagine it was *that* bad, but then I hadn't been Carmen's friend. I asked, "And this happened to Mel?"

"That's right. She and Mel had been best friends for a while. It was kind of an odd pairing, but I think Carmen enjoyed the sycophantic aspect of the friendship. Mel is very different from Carmen—sort of socially awkward, very sweet. And earnest. Carmen was . . . well, you know."

I did indeed. She could be quite cutting, sarcastic, smug, and definitely not awkward in any sense of the word.

"Anyway, something changed with their relationship recently. Something on Carmen's end. I don't know what it was, but suddenly Carmen was ignoring Mel's texts and phone calls and would roll her eyes when talking about her." He tilted his head to one side and looked worried. "Mel seemed really upset by it. In fact, she came to talk to me about it, but I said that I couldn't be caught in the middle of it all. Surely Mel didn't get angry and shove Carmen down the stairs?"

I didn't answer and he shook his head. "Never mind. That would be crazy." He seemed flustered suddenly. "Thanks for letting me do a brain dump with you. I guess librarians have to put up with all kinds of stuff, don't they?"

I gave him a reassuring smile. "I was happy to listen. Again, I'm really sorry about Carmen."

Elliot nodded and walked absently out of the library. After finding a vase and carefully arranging the flowers at the front of the library, I headed to the circulation desk to come up with a plan for Fitz's advice column. This plan, like all plans involving the cat, started with a picture of Fitz. I looked at him thoughtfully. I remembered there was a small pair of glasses in a closet that belonged to one of the puppets we sometimes used for storytime.

I hurried off to get them and carefully put them on Fitz's face, peering at him to see if he objected to the intrusion on his face. He beamed up at me as if he'd been waiting for spectacles his entire life. His looks were being totally exploited for the library's benefit, but Fitz seemed absolutely elated about the exploitation. He purred loudly and his lips turned upward for the camera as soon as I lifted my phone.

"Fitz," I said, "you're wasted as a library cat. You should have been a model for cat food commercials."

Fitz mewed his agreement as I continued snapping pictures. Then I took a look at what I had while the cat proceeded to take another nap. I found one picture where Fitz looked both intellectual and knowing and also completely captivating and favorited it.

Then I found some scrap paper and drafted a copy for the library flyers and social media posts about the advice column. Since Wilson definitely seemed to want the column to focus not only on our usual patron questions (how do I open a new email account, how do I get books on my e-reader, can you help me work the copier) but also on personal questions, I made sure to give examples of all the types of questions that a patron might have.

Then I buckled down on the research. I wanted to compile a list of credible, legitimate resources as references to help with the variety of problems that might be sent in. I had the feeling that, otherwise, I was going to be quickly in over my head.

I took a look at it after I was done. "Ask Fitz" was the banner I'd created with Fitz looking adorable. Wilson was right—this was a great way to generate interaction with our patrons as well as hopefully help a few out.

I found him in his office and showed him what I'd put together. He beamed. "That's perfect. Exactly what I was looking for. Now, can you go ahead and post it on social media? If you can also print out copies to put on the circulation desk and tables around the library. Then we'll see what we get in."

"And you'd like me to sort through them and pull out the most interesting to respond to?" I asked.

Wilson was already delving back into whatever work he'd been doing before I came in. He shrugged. "Let's see how it goes. If you get a huge number of responses, then yes, those can be winnowed down. But it might be nice to personally respond to as many of them as possible, even if the answers don't end up going on social media."

I considered this for a second. "The only problem with that is that I won't be able to individually reach out to patrons unless they've left their contact information. And I think a lot of the time, their questions may end up being anonymous."

Wilson said briskly, "We'll play it by ear. See how it goes. And thanks, Ann."

It was definitely a dismissal, so I left and carefully closed the door to his office behind me.

I ran into Luna on her way to the breakroom.

"Everything okay?" she asked. "You were having a pretty long conversation with that patron."

I nodded. "He was leaving a tribute to Carmen."

"Makes sense. By the way, since you saw Grayson last night, how was he doing? He must be pretty upset," said Luna.

"He was. I think he and his sister must have had a pretty good relationship. He was trying to find out more about what happened."

"Not that we know anything," said Luna. She frowned. "At least, I don't *think* we know anything."

"The only thing I noticed was that Carmen seemed to have been hit on the back of the head. But we found her face-down, so I don't think she got the injury from hitting her head on one of the stairs," I said.

Luna sighed. "Whatever happened, she didn't deserve it. And I still feel bad about everything."

"You shouldn't feel guilty about Carmen. She had a really difficult personality and that might have somehow contributed to her death. If we don't tell Burton about it and we say that butter wouldn't melt in her mouth, then he's going to have no idea that she was so abrasive. He wouldn't be able to search for her killer in any of the right directions."

"What do you think *are* the right directions?" asked Luna. "It sounds like you're saying that Carmen was killed by somebody close to her. Or, at least, somebody who knew her well and knew that she was . . . difficult. I like your word for her."

"It must have been someone close to her, right? I can't imagine that there was some opportunistic stranger who just suddenly decided to murder Carmen out of the blue. Maybe that happens some places, but it seems really unlikely to happen in a town like Whitby," I said.

"What did this guy say? The patron you were speaking to? He's Grayson's friend, you say? I know I've seen him in here before," said Luna.

"He was dating Carmen," I said.

Luna frowned. "I thought that guy who drove up in the truck yesterday was dating Carmen. At least, that's what it looked like. Although I ordinarily wouldn't have put the two of them together. He was sort of rough around the edges and she looked like a prom queen."

I said, "I think she was dating them *both*."

Luna's eyes were wide. "And they were okay with that?"

"I don't think so. From what Blake Thompson was telling me, Carmen was meeting Elliot for lunch to break up with him."

Luna said, "Yeah, I don't really see her with a guy like Elliot, either. He seems too polite and too academic for her." She paused. "Wait. Did you say she was having *lunch* with him to break up? I bet the restaurant customers must have loved that.

In a town this size, a public breakup would have been fodder for gossip for weeks."

I nodded. "That's what Blake thought, too. He said Elliot was very upset about it when he was driving by. But Elliot didn't mention anything about it to me. He acted as if they were still in a relationship."

Luna shrugged. "Maybe for him, they *were* still in a relationship. Maybe he thought he could somehow fix things and they'd be able to continue seeing each other. Could have been a little denial going on there. What else did he say? Or what did Blake say? And how on earth did Carmen end up dating *two* guys when you and I can't even find a single eligible person to go out with in this town?"

I gave her a wry smile. "Well, when you have women dating multiple men, it definitely doesn't help with the availability factor." I started to tell Luna about what Elliot had said about Mel, but then I stopped as a vague memory came back to me. "Ah, don't you have a friend named Mel? Mel Trumbull?"

"Sure! She comes to see me in the children's section about once or twice a week. We go out to lunch sometimes, when I'm not trying to save money. Which means our lunch dates lately are few and far between," said Luna, making a face. "Maybe she needs to pack a bag lunch and meet me in the breakroom."

I paused and Luna stared at me. "You're not saying that *Mel* has something to do with this! But she and Carmen were friends. Like *real* friends. Carmen was probably Mel's best friend."

I said lightly, "I'm not saying Mel had anything at all to do with Carmen's death. You asked what Elliot had said and that's what he mentioned. That Mel and Carmen had been at odds with each other lately. Had you noticed anything like that?"

Luna frowned. "I hate to say it, but I think I've been a little more self-involved than usual. I know Mel was talking to me about Carmen, but I thought she was just piling on."

"Piling on?" I asked.

"Yeah. You know, when your friend starts complaining about somebody and you say: 'I know what you mean! She can really be a pain!' That sort of thing."

I said, "So you just thought that Mel was being supportive when you were saying bad things about Carmen."

Luna sighed. "Things I now really regret, considering what's happened. But yeah."

"Did you ever see the two of them together? How they got along together?" I asked curiously.

Luna grimaced. "Not really. That's because, whenever Carmen walked up, I usually tried to be heading in the opposite direction. But one time when I was out running an errand, I did. The dynamics there weren't so hot. Carmen was definitely in charge, but then she was *always* in charge. I could see that she was bossing Mel around about something. It also looked like Carmen was putting Mel down somehow. Like in a passive-aggressive way." She shrugged. "That's not the way a friend should be. So Mel and I started hanging out a little more. In fact, she should be in the library soon . . . said she was going to run by on her way over to work."

I said, "I might come over to the children's section and introduce myself."

"Knowing Mel, she might introduce herself on the way in. She called me last night and was really upset about Carmen. I think she has conflicted feelings about her and probably feels guilty like I do. Anyway, I think she wanted to kind of talk the whole thing through. She *wanted* to talk it through last night, but I persuaded her to come by today in the hopes it would be quiet here. I needed to talk to my mom last night. After I did that, I was all talked out and really just wanted to veg in front of my TV until I fell asleep." She grinned at me. "I'm sure you went home and read most of *Ulysses*."

I snorted. "I think you know I *didn't* go home and read *Ulysses*."

Luna gave me a mischievous smile. "I made a shocking discovery in the breakroom. It appears that you're cheating on James Joyce with Rosamunde Pilcher."

I sighed. "You're right about that. *September* is sort of a comfort read for me."

"But from where you've bookmarked it, it looks like you were extracting comfort even *before* everything happened yesterday."

I grinned at her. "I needed comfort after reading *Ulysses*."

"I don't know why you just didn't tell your film club friend that you'd already read it. Then he wouldn't have kept pestering you to read the book. And he'd have believed you, because you've read *so many* books."

I said, "Because he would have wanted to discuss it in-depth and I only have a basic working knowledge of it. This guy has read the book multiple times."

"Next time, you should pick an easier book to read. Like *Infinite Jest*," said Luna with a snort. She glanced over to the children's department. "Okay, I should head over there. Do you want me to put some of the Fitz flyers in the kids' area? Or are you specifically targeting the adult patrons' questions?"

"I think Wilson wanted us to get a real mix, so let's go for it," I said.

"If you're ready to do some research on why the sky's blue," said Luna with a laugh.

# Chapter Six

D*ear Fitz,*
*I have a pretty quiet life, which I really like. But sometimes, I realize I'm a little bit lonely. Do you have any tips for an introvert for making friends?*

*Signed,*
*Solitary*

Dear Solitary,

Making friends can be a challenge for anybody. I was new at the library and made a lot of friends by just going up and hanging out with them. But that's easier for a cat than it is for a human. You don't have to go up and talk to total strangers like I do … maybe there are people who you already know who you'd like to spend a little more time with. Ask them questions—humans love to talk about themselves. I'm including a list of library clubs and events that might give you the perfect chance to meet people. I know you'll do claw-some at this!

Your Friend,

Fitz

LUNA WAS RIGHT ABOUT Mel. She came in about twenty minutes later and walked right up to the circulation desk. Fortunately, the library was quiet then or else it might have been tough to talk to her privately.

Mel introduced herself, holding out her hand. She had an anxious, restless demeanor, but her smile was genuine and went all the way up to her eyes, which were still swollen from crying.

"It's good to actually meet you," she said. "I feel bad because I've seen you in here for years and never really introduced myself."

I smiled back at her, "It's good to meet you now. And don't worry about it. The library isn't necessarily a social place."

Luna walked up as Mel said, "It's the best place in the world, isn't it? You can come to relax and be quiet and not speak to a soul. Or you can come in and talk to people and make friends and join clubs."

Luna grinned. "It's different things to different people."

Mel glanced around and said to me, "Is it okay if we talk for just a minute or two? That is, you don't have something else you should be doing?"

"It's fine," I said. "Technically, it's time for my break. I'll just spend it hanging out with you."

"Okay, good," breathed Mel in relief. "I'm sorry to make you two go through your story again. But I couldn't sleep a wink last night and until I know what happened, I'm thinking I won't get much sleep any other night. Carmen and I were good friends." She colored a little.

Luna waved her hand at me. "Ann, why don't you tell her? I wasn't there the whole time and I think you have a better perspective on the whole thing. But let's move over to the children's section so I'm technically still where I'm supposed to be working."

I did tell the story, being as undramatic and level as I possibly could. But still Mel's face was pinched with anxiety and she cried out uncontrollably at the part when I explained how I'd seen Carmen at the bottom of the stairs.

Mel's eyes were huge as I finished and tears pooled at the bottom of them, threatening to spill over. Luna was already thrusting tissues at her since the children's department had boxes on the tops of every group of shelves in an impossible attempt to keep germs at bay.

Mel dabbed at her eyes and cleared her throat a few times while looking at the floor. Then she said, "I hate this. Who could have done something like this?" Then she snapped her mouth shut as if she'd had an idea.

Luna frowned at her. "What's up, Mel? It looked like something came to mind just then? Or was it some*one* who came to mind?"

Mel shook her head and her brown hair fell across her face as she looked down at the floor again. "It's nothing. At least, I guess it's nothing."

I'd have let that go because clearly Mel didn't want to say anything. But Luna being Luna, she pressed a bit harder, leaning forward and looking at her friend with concern. "Mel, there's something on your mind. You're with friends."

Mel sighed. "It's just that Carmen and I had been arguing about something lately. I feel just awful about it."

Luna said quickly, "No one knew Carmen was going to be taken from us so suddenly . . . you shouldn't feel badly about an argument. After all, friends squabble." I saw an indecipherable expression pass across Luna's features for a second before giving Mel a reassuring smile.

Mel hesitated and glanced around them before saying in a low voice, "It's just that I didn't really approve of how Carmen was living her life."

"In what way?" I asked quietly.

Mel made a face. "She was dating a lot. And cheating on people."

Luna said, "We already heard she had two boyfriends at once."

Mel said, "Not just two. Three. At least, three that I knew about. And they really *didn't* know about each other. At least, two of them didn't know about each other until very recently and then they *were* mad when they found out, even though Carmen said she never planned on being exclusive to any one person. They were both arguing with Carmen to break up with the other guy. But nobody really knew about the third guy," said Mel.

"Who was the third guy?" I asked in a hushed voice.

Mel said miserably, "The mayor."

"What?" chorused Luna and I.

Luna continued, "The mayor? But he's married."

"That's what we were arguing about," said Mel sadly. "It's one thing for Carmen to be seeing two men at the same time and sneaking around. But I thought it was something completely different for her to be seeing someone who was married."

Luna gaped at her. "Carmen and the mayor? He's not even her age. What was the attraction there?"

Mel shrugged and looked embarrassed for Carmen. "That's the thing. I guess maybe because it was a challenge and Carmen always met challenges head-on? Maybe it was a thrill for her to do something illicit? She never gave me a good answer."

I said, "And you told her how you felt?"

Mel sighed. "I did. I really did. At first, I told myself it was none of my business and I didn't need to get involved. But it bothered me. For one thing, it was totally pointless. It wasn't like she was in love with Howard or anything. The only thing that could possibly have come of their affair was the end of his marriage."

Luna snorted. "And not only that, but the whole thing was just wrong. Carmen wasn't exactly experiencing a shortage in terms of the number of men she was dating."

Mel nodded eagerly. "That's exactly what I'm saying. Carmen could probably go out with any guy in town that she wanted to. So why would she pick somebody who was married? Somebody who was about twenty or more years older than she was? I couldn't believe it. It just seemed really unscrupulous to me and there came a point where I couldn't keep my opinion to myself anymore."

I asked, "So her relationship with the mayor had been going on for some time?"

Mel said, "Not *really* long, but a few months."

Luna said, "How did she even get to know him?"

Mel said, "Well, he's out and about a lot. And I know he does all of those 'Muffins with the Mayor' here at the library. I mean, she didn't tell me how they became acquainted, but I bet it was here."

Luna said, "Well, that surprises me. I guess people in power must have a certain draw."

I said, "But power in Whitby isn't really the same, is it?"

Mel said, "I'm not sure what she was thinking. But we never really totally made up after our argument. It's the one time I actually pushed back and told her I thought she was in the wrong." She gestured at Luna. "This is why I've become friends with Luna. She's so laid-back and easy to be around."

I said, "And Carmen could be difficult."

Mel nodded. "That's right. She liked having her own way. She didn't appreciate being told no. And she was always so uptight about everything. Hanging out with Luna is a relief. Everything Carmen did had ulterior motives. Luna's always totally upfront about everything. I don't have to worry she's sneaking off behind my back and talking about me to other people."

Luna looked uncharacteristically at a loss for words

"I feel so awful about her poor brother, too. I mean, he moved down here to be closer to her and now she's gone." Mel's mouth drooped. "Do you know Grayson?"

Luna shot me a sideways glance and I cleared my throat. "Only a little. He comes in the library sometimes. And he's my neighbor, too—he lives right down the street from me."

Mel sighed. "He's had a hard time lately and now this."

"What kind of a hard time?" asked Luna.

"His girlfriend broke up with him just recently. And now he's losing his sister on top of it all."

Luna's eyebrows shot up and she gave me a meaningful look when the girlfriend was mentioned. I gave her a slight, remonstrative shake of my head.

Mel said, "Anyway, thanks for telling me what happened. Carmen was my friend—my best friend—for a long time. I feel terrible. I wish we had been on better terms in the last few days."

Luna muttered, "You're not the only one."

Mel glanced at her watch. "I better head off to work. Good seeing you two."

As she left, Luna said, "So I'm going to dwell on the only good news I've heard for a while since life stinks otherwise. Sounds like Grayson is single again."

I felt myself color. "Maybe, but I don't think he's exactly in a romantic frame of mind right now. Plus the fact that he and I don't even really know each other."

Luna said, "Give it time." She paused. "I do really like Mel, but I have to wonder about her friendship with Carmen. I can't imagine the two of them had much in common."

I said, "Maybe opposites attract in friendships, too."

Luna shrugged. "Maybe so. I guess Mel might have also given Carmen the attention she always seemed to need, too. Every time I saw them together, it looked like Mel was hanging on Carmen's every word. Okay, well, on to work. How are things going on the Fitz front?"

We walked over to the circulation desk together and I showed her what I'd set up so far. Luna, as usual, was enthusiastic. She always made everyone feel good about their projects at the library. "I think it's going to be a hit. Although who knows what kinds of questions Fitz is going to get?"

"I know," I said dryly. "And Wilson seems to have put me in charge of the project. But he said the column itself could be a group effort. I may need your help to come up with appropriate responses for some things."

Luna said, "Sure thing, but I doubt you'll need to. You're a librarian! You have all the answers at your fingertips."

I said, "Except maybe when it comes to relationships. And I have the feeling this is the kind of setup where we'll get a lot of lovelorn messages."

Luna made a face. "Oh, I didn't really think about that. Relationships—ack. Well, between the two of us, we should be able to figure it out. Even though we're both single and not currently dating anyone."

The rest of the day flew by, which was a relief. The day before had been so awful and unsettling that I was worried there might be some dead time, and my mind might wander back to the moment I'd found Carmen at the bottom of the stairs. It was my turn to close up the library for the night, so it was nine-thirty by the time I told Fitz goodnight and got into my car and headed home to fall into bed.

The next morning, I packed my lunch and headed back out again. Luna came up to me in the parking lot before we walked in.

"You know what today is, don't you?" she asked a bit breathlessly.

I froze. "It's not Wilson's birthday or something, is it? I always manage to forget that."

"No, no. It's Muffins with the Mayor. The *mayor*," repeated Luna excitedly.

I unlocked the library door and we walked in to be greeted by a purring Fitz who wound himself immediately around my legs until I reached down and rubbed him. Then I gingerly picked him up, regardless of the fact I was getting orange and white fur on my clothes. "I remember the whole conversation about the mayor, Luna. But I'm not sure what we're supposed to do. We can't exactly accost Howard at our workplace and accuse him of having an affair with a trustee. And then intimate that perhaps he wanted her murdered."

Luna wasn't at all deflated by this. "Are you sure? There must be a way to *delicately* do that. A polite way."

I snorted. "I seriously doubt it. But maybe we can pick up some information." Fitz lovingly bumped his face against my jawline.

"Or, at least, *you* can. I'm the one who's stuck in the children's area with the storytime, remember? Come on, Ann. We owe it to Carmen to try and figure it out. At least, *I* owe it to Carmen."

I wasn't completely convinced we really owed anything to Carmen, but Luna certainly believed it. Plus, there was clearly a bit of guilt Luna still harbored inside her that she was wanting to relieve.

The community room of the library was a handy space. It was also used for storytimes, but because of the mayor's event, Luna was planning on gathering the kids in a corner of the children's section. The nice thing about the room was it could be used for anything the library needed. Today, we were setting out a few chairs and a long table. The mayor, Howard James, usually liked to mingle with the townspeople instead of being separated from them by a podium. His point each time was that he wanted the room to be ready for *conversations*.

As usual, he showed up early while I was still pulling out chairs. He laid down the boxes of muffins and doughnuts, greeted me by name with a hearty handshake, and then took the chair out of my hands and moved it himself. He was a big man with silver hair and a large grin. He was, I'd always reflected, the perfect politician. He could talk to absolutely anybody and find either common ground or something interesting to talk about.

Howard finished putting the chairs out and then spotted Burton, our police chief and went over to speak with him.

It was usually the same group of constituents who came in every week. Some of them were possibly tempted by free pastries. Others seemed to be trying to convince the mayor he needed to take action on a particular problem they faced in their neck of the woods—there was one man who always showed up to complain about his neighbor's tree. To his credit, Howard would always act as if it was the first time he'd ever heard the story of the tree. He had the gift of making you feel as if you were the only person in the world and he had all the time to listen to you. I could see where that could be an attractive quality and maybe that was part of what Carmen had been drawn toward.

A few people filed in, speaking with the mayor and getting muffins and juice. I turned to see Linus Truman, one of my favorite senior citizens, standing hesitantly at the door and walked over to speak with him. Linus had, until very recently, been our most private regular patron. For years, he'd come to the library daily and had a very particular pattern to his day there. He'd arrive, wearing a spotless suit and his owlish-looking glasses and sit down with the local newspaper before moving on to fiction, then nonfiction, then to lunch, before returning to the library and finishing up his day with *The New York Times*. Although he'd always been perfectly polite, he'd never engaged in conversation with me until Luna had gotten him to open up.

He gave me a shy smile as I approached him and cleared his throat. "Just thought I'd see the mayor this morning while I'm in the library."

I said, "Would you like me to introduce you?" Considering how religiously he kept to his routine, I thought this deviation must be huge for him.

He shook his head quickly. "No, thanks. Just here to observe. Maybe I'll speak with him next time."

"And hopefully to eat some muffins." I smiled. "Because otherwise they end up in the breakroom and I eat far too many of them."

I heard the mayor call my name from behind me and excused myself.

Howard's face was serious and he said quietly, "I've been out of touch the last twenty-four hours because I was out of town. A resident mentioned something about a tragedy here yesterday. Can you fill me in?"

"Of course," I said, taking a deep breath. Wilson would want this incident downplayed as much as possible, I knew. But from what Mel had told Luna and me about Howard's relationship with Carmen, this might come as a shock.

I started out cautiously, "We had a library trustee here yesterday, helping to prepare for the Friends of the Library book sale. We keep books for the sale in the basement and they needed to come up to the main floor to be placed on carts for the public to see."

Howard nodded. "Those are steep stairs. Who was the board member?" he asked, a note of urgency in his voice.

I swallowed and said, "Carmen King."

Howard blanched and his eyes widened. "And she fell down the stairs while getting the books?"

I shook my head slowly. "I'm afraid it's worse than that. It did appear, at first glance, to be an accident. But the police determined it wasn't. They've opened an investigation."

"You mean . . . murder?" asked Howard in a hushed voice as he glanced quickly around to ensure no one was moving closer. Beads of perspiration popped up on his forehead as he looked intently at me.

# Chapter Seven

"That's what I understand," I said quietly.

He paused for a moment and his color changed from pasty white to red and blotchy. He took a deep breath and said, "Do the police have any ideas in terms of who might be behind it? I mean, did you get a sense of the direction their questions were going in when they were talking to you?"

Linus was looking at Howard and me with interest before politely lowering his eyes when he noticed I'd seen him.

I said, "I wouldn't say I necessarily picked up on any type of direction. I'm guessing the police use pretty general questions when they're trying to figure out what's happened. I was asked how well I knew Carmen and if I'd known of her having any problems with anyone here at the library or elsewhere. And about her personal relationships."

Howard nodded, looking down at the floor. "And did you know any of those things?" He added quickly, lest I wonder over his interest, "It's just that this is big news for Whitby. Murders don't happen very often here, especially in our library, which is a favorite place for everyone in town. I want to make sure the townspeople feel secure."

I asked, "Did you know Carmen?"

Howard said, seeming flustered, "Not well, no. I feel badly about that. I'm trying to make an effort to get to know some of my younger constituents."

I smiled benignly at him to encourage him to speak more. In my head, I was thinking he'd certainly succeeded in getting to know one of his younger constituents, if what Mel had said was true.

He continued, "We'd engage in conversation sometimes, just as you and I are now. It's good to have a finger on the pulse of the younger folk in town. I'd like Whitby to continue being attractive to a variety of different age-groups and to find out how best to make that happen."

I nodded. "So you were getting ideas on that from Carmen."

He looked relieved. "Precisely! Aside from that, I didn't know her well."

I nodded again and said, "To answer your question, I didn't really know the answers to many of the questions. Like you, my relationship with Carmen was strictly business."

Howard flushed again and had the grace to look away. He said, "Well, perhaps Burton will find out it *was* an accident, after all. It must be hard to get an immediate read on these things." He glanced over at the clock across from him and gave me a broad smile. "Thanks, Ann. And good to see you! I suppose I should make myself available to some of the other folks."

He walked over to the food table and immediately started speaking with a young man who seemed to have a question about finding a job.

I poured out several cups of orange juice and set them on the beverage table. Then I walked back over to Linus.

"He's very approachable if you have a question or a concern," I said in an offhand way, hoping not to run Linus out of there.

He gave me a small smile and shook his head. "I might be more interested in the pastries," he confessed. "That bakery is one of my favorites."

I chuckled. "Well, whatever the draw, I'm glad you're here."

"Is attendance always this strong?" asked Linus, looking rather bemused. He took a step backward to get a little closer to the wall as a swarm of people of different ages wandered in.

"Not always. But there are frequently a good number of attendees. I guess it's just well-known, since the mayor has been regularly doing these meet-and-greets for years," I said. Since Linus was still looking uncomfortable, I added, "Can I pick up some food for you? Doughnuts? Muffins? Orange juice?"

He looked relieved and told me a couple of muffins and a drink would be good. I maneuvered my way to the refreshments table.

A minute later, I handed the drink and muffins to Linus who gave me a grateful smile and then looked a little awkward as if wanting to both eat and carry on a conversation and not entirely sure how to manage either one.

I was about to save him by making an excuse and walking away when he brightened and said, "Tell me what you've been reading lately."

Our common denominator was definitely books. I smiled at him and said, "What I'm *reading*, or what I'm *supposed* to be reading?"

"Now I'm intrigued," he said and happily took a bite of his apple-cinnamon muffin. He didn't even seem to notice more people had filed in, the room had become a bit more crowded, and the mayor had gotten louder and jollier, which likely would have bothered Linus under ordinary circumstances.

I tried to give him a somewhat entertaining version of my reading quandary. "You remember film club, of course. Well, there's one particular patron in there who is very enthusiastic about James Joyce."

Linus's eyes crinkled as he smiled. "I'm assuming you're speaking in particular of *Ulysses*."

"Exactly. So each time I've seen him, which is regularly, he's asked me if I've read his favorite yet. For a while, I had excellent excuses why that wasn't so. There were special events to prepare for here at work and then there were other books I was reading. But, as time went on, those excuses started to wear thin and I decided I needed to read the book. I'm a librarian, after all."

Linus asked solemnly, "How many times have you had to renew it?"

"Twice, I'm afraid. And, since that's the renewal limit, I had to return it and then check it out again." I confessed. "Fortunately, there wasn't a waiting list for the book."

"So what are you *actually* reading, then?" he asked curiously as he finished off his muffin.

"*September* by Rosamunde Pilcher." I chuckled. "I read it fairly regularly and especially when I'm feeling any sort of stress."

Linus tilted his head to one side. "*Ulysses* is stressful?"

"Oh, no. No, it's fine, it's just not holding my interest. There are some things going on at the library that have been stressful. So anyway, I'm now trying to hold myself to reading at least ten pages a day of Joyce's book and then consoling myself with Pilcher," I said.

He nodded as he carefully threw away his paper plate and took a sip of his orange juice.

I said, "At any rate, I'll have *some* progress to report when film club rolls around again in a couple of days."

Linus's expression suddenly changed to one of concern. "I read about the trustee who fell down the stairs here." He hesitated. "I must have been at lunch when it happened. When I came back by the library, it was closed for the day. I'm hoping you weren't one of the librarians who discovered her."

I gave him a smile. "Thank you, Linus. Unfortunately, I was. It was a real shock but I'm feeling a bit better today. I just feel terrible about Carmen."

He nodded. "I think I remember who she was. She was in here a lot, wasn't she? And *I'm* in here a lot, I suppose." He looked rueful. "She seemed very . . . efficient."

I was relieved Linus hadn't put me in the position of having to once again say bad things about a deceased trustee. "She was indeed. Carmen was *extremely* efficient."

Wanting to change the subject, I was about to ask Linus what he was reading (he always seemed to be juggling several books at one time) when I heard the unexpected sound of arguing behind me.

Linus's eyes widened a little and I gave a quick glance behind me to see Blake Thompson, one of Carmen's love interests, was engaged in a heated discussion with the mayor. Or, actually, he was *trying* to engage. The mayor appeared to want nothing to do with an argument.

"Not here," muttered Howard. "For heaven's sake, man. Get ahold of yourself."

Blake said, "Well, when you don't return my phone calls or emails, what am I supposed to do? At least I knew you were going to be here this morning. I don't have a lot of choice, do I?"

Howard quickly said, "I'll call you later today. Not now. This isn't the place."

Blake's voice was ragged and said, "I'm going to hold you to that. Look, I've had a really bad last twenty-four hours. I'm not going to put up with this on top of it all."

I hazarded a look at Blake and saw he looked just as ragged as he sounded. Carmen's death had apparently really thrown him for a loop. I suspected he was wearing the same clothes I'd seen him in the day before.

"I'll call you, Blake," said Howard in a calm voice. "Now, can you let me get back to my event, please?"

A moment later, I saw Blake striding out of the room and Howard chatting lightly to some of his constituents.

I turned back to Linus who said quietly, "That was interesting. An unscripted moment from the mayor."

I nodded and replied in my best, quietest, librarian voice, "You're right. We don't usually see the mayor at anything but his very best."

Linus was still subtly watching the mayor, his large eyes taking him in. "I have to wonder what that might have been about.

I ordinarily wouldn't have thought those men would have business together."

I thought about Blake's connection to Carmen. I wouldn't have put the two of *them* together, either. I shook my head. "It's a mystery."

Linus seemed ready to change the subject. "What's going to be featured at the next film club meeting?"

I smiled at him. "Might I be able to convince you to go?" Linus was definitely interested in most of the movies we showed at the library. Fortunately, I'd been able to present a great range of films and had terrific recommendations not just from other librarians, but from the club members, themselves. But I knew he had grown so used to his daily routines that it made it hard for him to join up with a group—any group—even for short periods of time.

Linus quickly said, "You know I'd enjoy it. It's just fitting it into my schedule. But I like hearing about it."

"Don't ever feel under any pressure to come. That's the nice thing about this particular library group—it's so laid-back. Except, maybe, when it comes to following up on book recommendations," I added wryly. "And I thought it might be fun to add a little mystery to the mix this month. We're going to watch that old noir classic: *Laura*."

Linus's eyes brightened. "An excellent choice. I'll have to see how things go that day." He turned to toss away his orange juice cup and then said, "Think I'll head over to periodicals to read for a while. Good to see you."

I was watching the mayor again and didn't notice when one of my nemeses entered the room. Zelda Smith was an older lady with henna-colored hair who lives in my neighborhood. She seemed to have an unerring radar when it came to tracking me down. I'd wistfully hoped she hadn't spotted me and that I could stand in an inconspicuous place in the room, but then I saw her eyes narrow as they locked in on me.

One of Zelda's goals in life was to get fresh blood on the homeowner association board, which she headed. I had to hand it to her: no matter how many times she might be turned down, she always ended up asking me again. Or asking me to reconsider. The problem was I was still trying to simply carve out personal time. Once I had a little free time from the demands of the library, I figured I could take on volunteering for the homeowner association board. It was a day I wasn't looking forward to. The board was reportedly fractious and there were lots of politics involved in terms of approving neighbors' requests. I braced myself and swiftly flipped through my catalog of excuses as Zelda squared her small shoulders and headed my way. As she stood in front of me, the smell of cigarettes (she was a notorious chainsmoker) automatically made me glance at her hands to ensure she hadn't brought in a contraband smoke into the hallowed grounds of the library. She hadn't.

"I was hoping I'd run into you, Ann," she said in her gravelly voice, eyes like bullets.

I held back a shudder and managed a rather sickly smile. "It was probably a good bet I'd be here. As I've mentioned, I spend a *lot* of time here." This was to counteract any pending requests for my participation on the board.

"Yes," said Zelda in a dry tone, "I've observed that. I'm guessing it cuts into your social life quite a bit, doesn't it?"

This was more than I'd hoped for. Zelda was finally catching on that I didn't have much time for anything outside of work. "Exactly!" I agreed quickly.

Zelda tilted her head, looking thoughtfully at me. "Dating and whatnot? That's not really happening, is it? No special friend?"

I thought we were going off on sort of an odd tangent, but I was so relieved not to have Zelda asking me again to join the homeowner association board that I happily nodded. "That's right, unfortunately." Although the pickings could sometimes be slim in Whitby, too. There were a lot of nice young men . . . it was simply that they were dating nice young women.

Zelda looked satisfied with her brief interview of me. "That's precisely what I'd gathered," she said briskly. "Which is why Kevin will be the perfect choice for you."

I blinked at her. "Kevin?" I asked in dawning horror.

"My nephew," said Zelda, narrowing her eyes again in irritation. She glared at me as if I hadn't been paying attention, although I was quite sure I had been riveted on her, waiting for the chance to refuse any board invitations. She continued, "You understand I would only ask the *highest* caliber person to go out on a date with him."

I was still trying to piece together exactly what she was talking about but alarm bells started ringing at the word *date*. "Naturally." I frowned in confusion.

"I *am* a little worried about your lack of civic engagement," she said severely.

"I always vote," I stubbornly answered. Why was I arguing? Why wasn't I telling Zelda in no uncertain terms that I wasn't wanting to date anyone now? Not, unless, by some happenstance, Grayson was suddenly free. And suddenly interested.

"I mean on the *neighborhood* level." Zelda pursed her lips.

I stared helplessly at her. Was I about to be hit with both barrels? Fixed up on a blind date *and* asked to join the homeowner association board? Would this conversation never end?

Zelda apparently decided to leave well enough alone. "Kevin is a wonderful boy. I want him to have the perfect visit to Whitby."

Now I felt a slight tingling of relief. "Kevin's not a permanent resident, then? Not a recent transfer?" Kevin would be *leaving* again. Excellent.

Zelda arched her eyebrows at me. "That remains to be seen."

I frowned at her.

Zelda sighed and briskly continued, "I believe Kevin is using this trip as a sort of reconnaissance mission. He'll come to Whitby, see what a pleasant town it is, have some enjoyable experiences, eat my wonderful cooking, and then decide to settle down here. Frankly, I could use the extra help every now and then with lifting things or cutting back bushes. And, of course, he's my favorite nephew." She gave me an arch look. "Perhaps he'll even be willing to help out with the homeowner association board. We *must* get younger people involved."

I glanced over at the mayor to see if he needed any help. Or wrangling. However, and very unfortunately, he appeared to be holding his own with no problem at all and was laughing merrily with a constituent who appeared to be telling him quite the fishing story.

Zelda intoned, "Think what will happen if the current trustees are unable to serve. There are any *number* of reasons why that might happen. Illness! Injury! Sudden and unexpected demise! The next thing you know, people in the neighborhood might let all of our carefully-crafted rules fly out the window. They might paint their houses purple or pink. They might throw raucous parties. They might allow farm animals to traipse through their front yards."

I glanced away again, more desperately this time. I saw Luna walking by the community room and realized she was likely trying to gauge when she might be able to use the room to set up for her next storytime, which was directly following the one that just wrapped up. I gave her a panicked look and she grinned at me and headed over.

"I'm so sorry," she said looking as chastened as she could. "Could I please borrow Ann for a few minutes? I need her help with something."

Zelda, fortunately for me, didn't spend very much time in the library and apparently hadn't met our colorful new employee. I wasn't sure if it was Luna's purple hair, her tattoos, or her piercings that startled Zelda, but I was grateful for the stunned silence Luna's appearance created.

"Zelda, it was good speaking to you," I said smoothly as I maneuvered myself away and marveled at my ability to fib.

"I'll call you to set up a time," she responded, suddenly regaining her voice.

I turned back around. "A time?"

"For Kevin to call you," said Zelda, rolling her eyes over my apparent forgetfulness. "I do have your number."

I wasn't sure exactly how she'd gotten it, but I supposed homeowner association presidents had their methods.

# Chapter Eight

I followed Luna out of the community room and leaned against one of the bookcases in the children's area outside it. "Thanks, Luna. I owe you."

"Homeowner association again, I presume," said Luna with a chuckle.

"Even worse. Homeowner association *and* a blind date with a visiting nephew named Kevin," I said, suddenly feeling very sorry for myself. I had been on many, many blind dates. They never seemed to go well. One of them in particular had gone horribly wrong.

"Glad I could rescue you," said Luna with a wink. She glanced at her watch. "Ugh. I guess we'll have to have storytime somewhere else."

A dry voice behind us answered, "Sorry. When Howard gets chatty, it can take a while."

We whirled around to see the mayor's wife, Tanya. She was tall and very thin with a sort of horsey, patrician bearing. As usual, she was very elegantly dressed with a silk blouse and linen skirt. I remembered she was considered 'old money' in Whitby and the large house the couple lived in was her family home.

Luna quickly said, "Oh, that's all right. With the really little guys, it's a good idea to shake storytime up. For the moms, too. Sometimes they haven't had enough coffee to stay awake. A change of location may make them more alert."

Tanya gave her a thin smile. "I'm sure that's true." Her voice said she couldn't possibly care.

Luna glanced at the clock and cheerfully said, "Time to read to the munchkins. Excuse me, please." She headed off toward a group of young children, but cast me a woeful look that said she hoped she hadn't upset yet another member of the library board.

I put on my best smile for our trustee. "There's lots of food still in the room. Would you like me to make a plate for you and bring it out here?"

Tanya raised an eyebrow in recognition and said, "Thanks, but no. I'm trying to stay away from carbs and sugar."

It appeared she'd quite successfully done so, and for quite some time. She was as thin as a rail.

I was about to excuse myself and find some shelving to do until the mayor's event was over when Tanya unexpectedly spoke again. "You're the one who discovered her, aren't you? Carmen?"

I nodded. "Yes," I said quietly. I glanced around, making sure none of the little ones getting ready for storytime were in the vicinity. If Tanya was about to question me about Carmen, it wasn't the type of story the children needed to be hearing. Fortunately, they were all busy with the picture books on the other end of the room.

She nodded back, thoughtfully. "I thought so. Such a pity." Her face reflected a different opinion than her words had.

I said carefully, "It was a tragedy. I suppose you knew Carmen well, being on the board together?"

Tanya gave a careless shrug. "I wouldn't say *that*. No, I wouldn't say that at all. Did anyone really know her well? She could be very cagey. Of course, we did serve on the library board and Friends of the Library together. I feel quite guilty about the fact she was gathering books for the Friends sale when she perished." Her face, again, contradicted her statement. "I couldn't make it to help her, you see."

I wasn't sure what to say to that and was still mulling over options when she continued. "She was very driven, very organized. I really don't know what the library will do without her. I'm sure there will be a void in leadership. Howard and I were shocked when we heard the news," she added drolly.

"It must have been a terrible surprise," I offered. "It's terrible when someone really young dies."

Tanya sat down on a bay window seat and stretched her long legs out. "Yes, yes it is. Very unnatural. Howard and I were at home when we heard the news and we both said much the same thing. That it was a shock and so awful. You know, when young people die." Again, her carefully-modulated voice didn't reveal any emotion whatsoever.

But there was something else I'd noticed. "You and your husband were at home?" I repeated.

"That's right," said Tanya. "It's been something of an adjustment lately. Howard has started this new routine where he works from home in the mornings and then is in the town hall office during the afternoons. At first I thought he was doing it simply to annoy me." This with an unexpected trilling laugh. "I considered the house my own personal territory in the mornings and had my own routine of exercising, puttering around the yard, and reading. It was something of an invasion when he changed his own daily routine."

"I can imagine that it would be," I said slowly, still considering the implications of Howard being at home with Tanya and not out of town, as he'd stated.

"Then he told me he felt he got more accomplished in a few minutes at home than he did in the office for hours. Apparently, lots of people drop in on him at the office." Tanya gave an expressive shrug indicating these people were somewhere below the level of local yokels.

"I'm sure it's meant a big shift for you and your own routines."

Tanya seemed to appreciate the sympathy. She said, "It has been, but it's worked out all right once I realized things were going to change for good. Now we take the dog for a walk together, eat breakfast together while answering emails and reading the paper, and then get some work done before Howard heads out the door. That's when someone called me about Carmen." She shook her head, whether over Carmen's fate or bothersome phone calls, I wasn't entirely sure. She frowned. "Actually, I believe I forgot to pass the message along to Howard."

I said, "Well, the police certainly seem to be on the case. I'm sure they'll get to the bottom of everything soon."

Tanya raised her finely-plucked eyebrows again. "Indeed? So it's as I heard? Murder?"

"I'm afraid so. The police have determined her fall wasn't an accident."

"Mercy," said Tanya, without inflection. "I wonder who could have done such a thing?"

"I wish I knew," I said, hoping maybe Tanya would offer some thoughts on Carmen's possible enemies. Or something helpful.

"And I haven't the faintest idea," she said, reaching into her tiny, expensive purse and pulling out her iPhone. The conversation was clearly over.

A few minutes later, the mayor's event was over. I went inside to clean up as the mayor walked out of the room, still talking to one of his constituents in a jolly tone. Fortunately, everyone who'd attended the event had been scrupulous about tidiness and besides removing the trash, there wasn't much to do, except attend to the leftover food.

The mayor, before leaving, stuck his head back in the room. If nothing else, he was always very polite. "Thanks for all your help with Muffins with the Mayor," he said earnestly. "Please feel free to take any of the leftover food and beverages to the breakroom for the staff to enjoy later, if you'd like."

I knew Wilson liked a customary shot of sugar with his lunch, so I nodded, smiling, at Howard. "I'll do that. Thanks."

I wiped the few crumbs that were on the serving table off into my hand and glanced up again, surprised the mayor was still there. "I'm sorry. Can I help you with anything? Are you on the calendar for the next event?"

He shook his head and said, "Oh, that's already been taken care of, thanks. No, but there was something I wanted to clarify. I'm afraid I misspoke earlier."

Howard really was a politician. And was apparently taking notes from some of the best in terms of his careful word-crafting. "Oh? I didn't realize," I said. Although I did. And I strongly suspected he'd spoken briefly with his wife after he'd stepped out of the room.

He cleared his throat and looked briefly away before looking back at me, eyes very direct. "That's right. I don't know what I was thinking of. It's been very busy lately, you see, and I think I'm getting my days mixed up. Actually, it was Tanya who reminded me we *weren't* out of town when poor Carmen fell. No, we were at home."

"I see" I nodded. "It can be easy to get days confused, can't it?"

The mayor slumped just a bit in relief and nodded eagerly. "Can't it? And life has been very different lately. I'm working from home in the mornings now. It's amazing how much more I can get accomplished there. At the town hall, I'm always dodging phone calls and drop-in visits."

"That's great," I said lightly. "And somewhat counterintuitive. I'd think working from home would be very distracting."

Howard chuckled. "Well, I'm a very disciplined person. The trick, you see, is simply to allow yourself to be distracted, but only at specific times and intervals. As a reward, of sorts. So I'll sit down and work on emails for thirty minutes, then I'll reward myself by checking social media or getting a snack or petting the dog."

I could see Howard was the mansplaining type, for sure. I made a point of smiling and nodding as if I was taking it all in. Wilson, I felt, owed me for my obsequiousness. I was starting to feel like Dickens's Uriah Heep.

"Sounds like a good way to stay productive," I said.

"For sure. You should give it a try some time," he said.

I successfully resisted the urge to point out I couldn't very well do much of my library work from home, unless it consisted of research.

"Well, better run. Thanks again for your help and do take that food to the breakroom. Can I give you a hand with it?" he quickly asked in the tone of someone who's expecting a refusal.

"I've got it, but thanks," I replied with the obligatory response.

A few minutes later, I was stacking up the boxes of muffins when I heard what sounded like an angry conversation below the cracked window of the community room. When I glanced through the window, Howard was angrily barking at Tanya, who looked as unflappable and icy as usual. I couldn't make out the words, but one thing was clear—this was the second time in the last hour or so that I'd heard Howard James lose his temper.

# Chapter Nine

D*ear Fitz,*
     *My employer doesn't seem to trust me to do a good job. But if he doesn't give me a chance, how can I prove I'm worthy of trust?*
     *Signed,*
     *Frustrated*

Dear Frustrated,

Just make sure you're the purrfect employee! Be on time and make sure you're not the first to leave. Volunteer for tasks no one wants to do. If nothing changes, schedule a meeting to talk about your concerns. Good luck! For further reading, I dug up some articles on having productive conversations with employers—check out the links below.

     Your Friend,
     Fitz

A few minutes later, I was putting a tray of muffins and doughnuts into the breakroom. Luna poked her head in, fresh from her storytime, and groaned when she saw it.

"I look at that tray and you know what I see?" she asked.

I shook my head with a grin.

"Sabotage," she answered. "Did I tell you I'm on a diet? My mom and I both are. I swear I don't know how the weight has just hopped right on me since I moved here. When I was in New York, I was *always* the same weight." She stared gloomily at the muffins.

"I'd blame the mayor, except he only has his Muffins with the Mayor event once a month," I said lightly. "Anyway, I don't see that you've gained any weight."

Luna wagged a finger at the tray. "Oh, it's there, believe me. You know what I think it is? It's lack of exercise. When I was in New York, I walked everywhere. Here, I'm just hopping in my car and carting myself over to the library and back."

"Same here," I said. "Although I'm not sure I particularly want to change my habit right now. It's about a hundred degrees outside."

Luna tilted her head to one side, letting her purple hair tumble. "I wonder if I could just *sweat* this weight off? Maybe I should start walking to work and back."

I gave her an encouraging smile, although it sounded miserable to me. I decided to offer an alternative. "Do you have a bicycle? That would be quicker and would still provide exercise."

Her eyes widened. "True! And no, I don't, but I bet I could find an inexpensive one online. Because I'm also trying to save money."

Wilson joined us in the breakroom. He was delicately holding Fitz, who was purring. He set the cat down carefully and I walked over and gave him a scratch under his chin. He gave me an appreciative look before finding his favorite breakroom sunbeam and falling asleep in it, still purring contentedly in his sleep.

Wilson's eyes widened as he spotted the tray of pastries. "Oh, wow." He got himself a plate and picked out a few muffins for himself. "Wasn't there a good turnout for the event?" he asked me with concern.

"There were plenty of people there, but I guess the draw was the mayor and not so much the food. Or else, the attendees weren't very hungry," I offered. I glanced at my watch. Considering the three of us were in the breakroom, I figured I should head out to the circulation desk.

"Before you go out there," said Wilson, brushing a few crumbs from his mouth, "I wanted to talk with you about the advice column."

Luna tried unsuccessfully to hide a smile. We'd talked before about Wilson and his pet projects. And this one really *was* a 'pet' project.

I walked back toward Wilson. "I should have given you a better update earlier. You probably saw the flyers and the signs on the bulletin boards here, but I also did post a cute picture of Fitz wearing glasses and a notice about the column on our social media accounts. We've had a couple of questions come in and I've answered them but haven't posted them yet."

Wilson nodded eagerly. "Yes, I've seen the social media posts. What I wanted to let you know is we've already gotten some responses. The column seems to be very popular online. It's even being *shared*."

I admit my heart sunk a little at this news. After all, I didn't exactly consider myself an expert when it came to relationships

. . . or even life. I was very good at doing research, but aside from that, I felt like I struggled. I still had a crush on a man who wasn't interested, for heaven's sake. And now I was apparently stuck with yet another looming blind date with someone named Kevin.

Luna leaned forward with interest. "What kinds of responses are we getting? I mean, what do the problems look like?"

Wilson gave her an approving look as if she were a star student. "The problems that I've seen come in are a range. Some of them are written by students and have to deal with telling parents about a bad grade or something similar. Some are definitely letters from the lovelorn."

I winced. Again, I wasn't feeling super-qualified to give advice for relationship issues right now.

Luna said to Wilson, "That's great that the program is getting such a response! But then, a lot of people don't really have anyone to go to when they have issues. Neutral parties can be very attractive because you know the replies aren't biased."

Wilson looked uncomfortable and suddenly directed his attention toward Fitz. This attention was somewhat unwarranted since Fitz was completely curled up in a ball in the sunbeam. "I don't know if replies from neutral parties *aren't* biased. I think our experiences have a tendency to color how we respond, even if we don't want them to."

I frowned. "I'm sorry—what are you saying? I thought perhaps Luna and I could even take turns responding to the Ask Fitz questions." I was sincerely hoping this was the case. "You'd mentioned earlier that responding could even be a group effort at the morning meetings."

Wilson sighed. "And now I've reconsidered that idea. It's just that Luna's experiences aren't exactly in the small-town realm."

Luna's eyebrows shot up. "But I grew up here!"

"And immediately left and spent most of your adult life in a big city with big city problems. I'm just not convinced you're the best person for this job," said Wilson. His voice didn't sound unconvinced at all—it sounded certain he didn't want Luna to have anything to do with it.

Luna looked as if she'd been slapped, although no one had been anywhere near her. "But having a lot of experiences is good for this kind of job. It helps me deal with different types of people. Even in a small town, there's not such a thing as a cookie cutter problem."

Wilson cleared his throat and stood, actions I knew indicated the discussion was over. "I'm afraid I don't see it quite the same way. Let's start out with Ann responding to the columns, for now anyway. If that needs to change, I'll re-evaluate. Ann, if you need anyone to consult with, you can feel free to ask Luna her opinion, but I want you to be *the* person behind this program."

As soon as he'd closed the door behind him, I quickly said, "I'm sorry about this, Luna. Wilson has been in a funny mood lately. Believe me, I don't want to be the person behind Ask Fitz. I'm with you—life experiences are key for dispensing advice and my life experiences are fairly minimal and random."

But Luna would hear nothing of it. She said, "You're completely wrong, Ann. You have more common sense in your little finger than most people have in their whole bodies. *That's* what you're bringing to the table—your brain. Maybe you haven't had as many life experiences as I have, but that's a *good* thing. Wilson is right: this column is intended for a particular audience. And the audience doesn't necessarily understand a New York state of mind."

I shook my head. I could tell Luna was still hurt, as she should be. It seemed like Wilson had stood in her way a lot lately, and I really couldn't figure out why. First there was the pay raise thing, which Luna had asked for and which hadn't gone well. Then he hadn't been at all flexible with Luna's hours when she'd asked him for some extra time to take her mom to appointments . . . causing Luna's mom to have to switch around some appointments. It was as if Wilson was determined to stand in her way, no matter what the issue was.

But Luna apparently read my features and the next thing I knew, she was rolling her eyes. "Please, Ann. Do you think I'm going to completely shy away from offering you advice for the advice column? Does that really sound like me? As soon as I get the chance, I'm going to be glancing through some of those entries to see what's on people's minds."

I still must have looked troubled because she said, "Besides, I've got a great idea for something, myself. You know how I've wanted to get more teens involved in the library?"

I nodded, happy to be getting on a slightly different subject. "Sure. For a good reason—historically, we haven't been able to lure as many teens here. It's tough to come up with a really good program for them. They're not exactly excited to come to the library for an art program and there hasn't been too much participation when we've tried book clubs."

Luna looked like she was warming to her subject. "Exactly! I want the library to be a fun place for these kids to come. But they don't have a lot of time. When I've talked to the teens who've come in, they're really strapped for time between school, jobs, sports, and trying to keep up with their friends. So I just casually started asking them what kind of program *they'd* like. What they'd find useful. They were saying they don't have study hall in school anymore. I mean, can you *imagine*?"

I didn't say I hadn't had study hall at Whitby High either. Apparently, it had been abolished at some point in the 80s.

"So I asked them if it would be helpful to have a study room set up, especially during exam weeks. We could have snacks and soft drinks and maybe even some music. Maybe we could even have a couple of off-duty teachers," said Luna, tilting her head to one side, thoughtfully.

I grinned at her. "Is there such a thing as an off-duty teacher? They're not exactly like off-duty cops."

She grinned back, but looked distracted. "So, what do you think?"

Luna was so eager that at first I couldn't bear to tell her it sounded a lot like our ill-fated study buddy program at the library a few years ago. After our youth librarian had stepped out of the (then-quiet) room, a food fight had erupted. When Wilson had seen the damage, he'd vowed to never host anything like that again. But maybe she needed to be clued in so she could avoid some of the issues we'd had last time.

I said slowly, "I think it sounds good. We had something *slightly* similar years ago, but it wasn't handled well. When you ask Wilson about it, make sure to tell him you plan on it being completely supervised by adults and the kids themselves requested it."

Luna beamed at me. "Good tips. I'll do that." Then she looked a little deflated. "Although getting it past Wilson is the big thing. He's turned into Dr. No lately, when it comes to me."

I had a feeling I knew why, too. Luna was a very industrious worker while she was at the library. And I knew Wilson has admired the rapport she has with the kids and their parents. She also was quite creative when it comes to program ideas. The only problem with Luna was that she had a habit of coming in late and needing to unexpectedly ask for time off. Wilson had always been a real stickler when it came to punctuality. I'd seen him make note of her lateness with pursed lips and an eye on the clock. I knew a lot of her lapses had to do with making sure her mom was settled in the mornings, but some of it had to do with Luna herself—and her laid-back approach to time and life.

I hesitated. The last thing I wanted to do right now was to point out what seemed obvious to me, but I also wanted Luna to get past this rough patch with our boss. I said, "You probably don't know this, but Wilson is super-strict about punctuality. Maybe you could try leaving a little earlier to get here? You might be doing this anyway if you're thinking about biking to work."

Luna's eyes opened wide as if she was hearing a revelation from above. "You mean the times I've been a little late? I haven't even been running that far behind."

It depended on what you called behind. To Luna, fifteen minutes was nothing. To Wilson, it was a huge deal. It hadn't created any problems because the times it had happened, I'd just floated between the children's section and the circulation desk. But it *could* have created problems.

Luna frowned. "But he hasn't said anything to me about it."

I nodded. "That's Wilson's way. He won't say anything . . . he just takes notes."

There was a determined jut to Luna's chin now. "Got it. Okay, so I'll come in early now. On my bike, once I get one. Now I'm motivated! I can make this happen." She looked at her watch. "Better run. Operation Perfect Employee is now underway." She saluted me and then scurried out of the breakroom.

# Chapter Ten

D*ear Fitz,*
        *Suddenly, I feel like I'm in middle school again. There's a woman I really like. I'd like to ask her out, but I'm not sure she likes me the same way. What should I do?*

*Signed,*

*Unsure*

Dear Unsure,

Nothing ventured, nothing gained! Make the opportunity to speak with her privately and ask her out for something casual—a coffee, maybe. That's when you might have the chance to find out how she really feels.

For more tips, check out the links below for experts' thoughts on asking for dates.

Your Friend,

Fitz

THAT AFTERNOON, I WAS at the circulation desk when we had a call come in. "Whitby Library, Ann speaking," I said.

I heard an educated drawl and straightened up a little. Tanya James was on the line. "Hi, Ann. This is Tanya James. I was wondering if you or someone else could give me a hand tomorrow with some books for the Friends sale."

"Of course we can help you out," I said automatically. I knew Wilson would automatically sign off for somebody to help out Tanya. "What time works best for you?"

"I'll have a few errands to run in the late morning, but I could meet you at my house around 12:30? Would that work?" She gave me the address, even though I knew exactly which house it was. There were only so many mansions in town, after all.

"That's perfect," I said smoothly. "See you then."

The rest of my day was a series of interruptions like that. I helped an older gentleman learn how to find his emails on his cell phone, helped a patron troubleshoot one of our more-finicky computers, and made a few book recommendations for a mom who was trying to get back to reading now that her kids were a little older.

In between, I hesitantly worked on Ask Fitz while Fitz lay complacently beside me on the circulation desk, not a care in his furry head. I was positive Fitz's answer to most of the questions posed would be a purring, "Relax! Go find a sunbeam and sprawl out in it."

Wilson had understated the response to Ask Fitz. I was stunned and rather overwhelmed to discover not only had the post had lots of views on social media, it had lots of responses. The questions did range, as Wilson mentioned, from the minor to the major. And it looked as if the post had been shared many,

many times. I wasn't sure quite what qualified as 'going viral,' but Ask Fitz seemed to be on the cusp.

I glanced up from cataloging and saw Burton walking up to the desk. "Read any good books lately?" he asked with a grin.

"Good ones and bad ones." I snorted.

"Uh-oh. What should I avoid? Got a tip for me?"

I said, "Skip *Ulysses* if you like your novels straightforward. I mean, I love William Faulkner and his stream of consciousness. But Joyce takes it to a whole new level."

Burton chuckled. "Got it. I'll make a mental note of that," he said, tapping his large forehead. "Although I don't think I was in danger of picking up James Joyce for any light reading."

I said, "*Are* you looking for a book recommendation? I can pull out some stuff I think you'd enjoy."

He shook his head. "Still trying to wade through a World War II novel I checked out, but thanks. I was just coming in to see how things were going here. The library seems to be at the center of these murders, unfortunately."

I snorted. "Better not let Wilson hear you say that. He's on a campaign to keep the library's reputation spotless."

Burton said, "And I totally understand that. I was just wondering if you had any information for me. I know a lot of people close to Carmen come in here a lot. *Carmen* was in here a lot, after all, as a trustee."

I said slowly, "Well, I've spoken with both Blake and Elliot. Both of them seem very upset about Carmen's death and convinced the other guy had something to do with it."

Burton nodded, "Especially Blake, I bet."

"Exactly."

"Since you seem to have some background with Blake, what do you make of him?" asked Burton.

I blew out a breath. "Well, I wouldn't say I had *much* background with him. I went to school with him and he helps out in the library from time to time with maintenance issues. With an old library, there are plenty of maintenance problems, as you'd probably guess. He's the kind of guy who's able to do anything. And if he can't do it, he can figure out how to."

Burton said, "Aside from his capabilities?"

I said, "I think he has a temper. I remember in school he'd get frustrated sometimes with classes and would kind of blow up." I paused. "You know, it's not really fair of me to judge somebody for something that happened when he was a teenager. I wasn't the same person then that I am now either."

"How about now, then?" asked Burton. "Have you seen any signs of temper still?"

"Blake seems really affable to me. He's eager to please; he has a good work ethic. He's cheerful. The only thing I'd say that I've noticed is the way he was really jealous over Carmen."

Burton nodded. "Carmen seems to have been quite an instigator. Do you think she liked the drama she created?"

I said dryly, "I have the feeling she might have. This is going to sound bad, but Carmen was all about Carmen. She probably loved having guys fight over her."

"Was that what was happening?" asked Burton.

I quickly said, "I didn't see anything like that. All I know is what I've heard from Blake and from Elliot. I know the two of them were squabbling over her. And I know the only time I've really seen a display of temper from Blake in recent memory was over Carmen. He's pretty convinced Elliot had something to do with Carmen's death. He probably told you the same thing."

Burton chuckled. "Yes. Numerous times. Fairly stridently. He can't seem to understand why I can't just drive over to the college and arrest Elliot."

"Lack of evidence."

"Exactly. An argument between Carmen and Elliot isn't exactly enough for me to lock Elliot up. There were no witnesses at the restaurant to say Elliot made threats against Carmen's life. He was merely upset, as most people would be."

I said quietly, "By the way, I heard something else. Were you aware Carmen and the mayor were having an affair?"

Burton nodded. "A neighbor mentioned it to me. Apparently though, not many people know about it. Although *you* seem to." He raised his eyebrows. "I guess the library really *is* an information hub."

Burton glanced around and continued in a carefully casual voice, "Say, is Luna around?"

I wasn't sure if I should keep pretending I didn't know Burton was interested in Luna or call him on it. So I said, "I think she's on her break, but she should be out soon. Want me to send her over your way?"

Burton hemmed and hawed for a moment and then looked helplessly at me. "You don't think Luna had anything to do with Carmen, do you?"

# Chapter Eleven

I blinked at him. Here I'd been thinking he was wanting to see Luna for personal reasons and he was worried about the case. "What makes you ask?"

He shook his head dismissively. "It's nothing. Just a feeling I got right after you both found Carmen. I got the impression she was holding something back from me."

I said staunchly, "No way. For one thing, Luna is a terrible liar. She doesn't appear to have the capacity to deceive anyone at all. And I don't think she has a violent bone in her body. She's always looking out for animals and won't even kill insects. She's a vegan. I just can't imagine a vegan as a killer."

Burton looked a little less certain that vegans couldn't be murderers, but he still seemed to breathe a sigh of relief. He gave me a quick look and then glanced away. "Okay, thanks. I'm sure you're right. There was something else I wanted to ask you, too. You don't happen to know if Luna is dating anyone, do you?"

I hid a smile and said, "I know for a fact she's not."

Now Burton's relief seemed even greater. "That's good. Even if it's a little surprising. I'm sure she's probably really picky about who she would go out with." His forehead puckered at the thought.

"Well, I think she looks out for herself, of course. But the truth is she's been really wrapped up with work and trying to get more engagement with teens at the library. And her mom keeps her busy, too."

Burton leaned in a little. "Engagement with teens? That's something my department is interested in, too. What kind of program is she thinking about?"

I said carefully, "It's nothing that's been approved by our director yet, at least as far as I'm aware. But Luna's really eager to host a study hall type event so kids can think of the library as a good place to get their work done. And, I guess, a relaxing and fun place too, because she wants to have snacks there and things like that."

Burton nodded. "Good ideas. Maybe it's something the police department could collaborate on: maybe we could even contribute to the cost of the food and drinks. We want to have an event to show the local police in a friendly light. I could speak to the director about it."

If the police were involved in the event, I was sure there would be absolutely no food fight happening. I said, "It would probably be good to speak with Luna first because I'm not sure she's approached Wilson yet about it. Then maybe the two of you could talk to him together."

Burton looked relieved. "Great idea, Ann. Thanks. And thanks for all the info." He hurried out the door with a backward look toward the children's area.

That night, I took Fitz home with me again just to have his company. He was, as always, the perfect guest—he contentedly watched me cook spaghetti for supper as if my work at the stove was fascinating (he was rewarded with a little bit of ground beef). Then he curled up next to me on the sofa as I struggled through my chapter (in this book, they're called 'episodes') of *Ulysses* before picking up my *September* book in relief. When I turned in, he silently jumped up on the other side of my queen-sized bed and politely gave me plenty of space as he curled up in a ball with his fluffy tail covering his face and purred loudly until we both fell asleep.

The next morning, I awoke with a start. Had I remembered to tell Wilson about Tanya James's request? I'd meant to, but then I'd gotten either pulled into helping a patron or into the Ask Fitz column. I squinted at the clock. I certainly wasn't going to call Wilson at six o'clock, although I knew he was probably up. He was probably already ensconced in his suit, for heaven's sake. I decided I could let him know once I got there. Because it was Tanya, he definitely wasn't going to reject her request.

When Fitz and I finally pulled up to the library, we were there about thirty minutes before it opened to the public. I raised my eyebrows and grinned in surprise as Luna laboriously pedaled up, wearing a backpack and a strained smile in response.

"I'm early!" she said, puffing out breath. "But I knew it was safe to come this early because you have a key and you're *always* early."

"And you're making me feel lazy for not exercising," I said. "Good for you! How did you end up with a bike?"

Luna was still trying to catch her breath. "Oh, I'd texted my mom yesterday after we talked about it. She knew a neighbor who was trying to downsize because her youngest left for college. Sure enough, she had a bike. Let me have it for ten dollars."

I was still getting the library key out of my purse (Wilson, always very rules-oriented and security-conscious, hadn't yet seen fit to give Luna one) when we heard a car pulling up behind us.

"Oh good," breathed Luna amid gasping breaths, "Wilson is here to witness my early arrival." She took the cat carrier from me so I could grab the key.

And indeed, we gave a quick wave to his astounded visage as he parked.

Luna followed me in and gently set the carrier down, crooning to Fitz as he pranced out of it and rubbed against her. "I wonder how many early mornings it will take before he sees I'm really committed," she mused.

I knew Wilson could be pretty stubborn and tended to cling to his opinions, but I didn't mention this. "Why don't you just take it one day at a time?" I asked.

Luna nodded. "And Mom mentioned she'd like to come spend the day here with me tomorrow. It's a good thing—she needs to get out of the house when I'm gone all day."

"And film club is tomorrow," I pointed out. "Didn't she really like it the last time she went? She seemed to."

Luna lit up. "She did! All right, that's a no-brainer then." She glanced back to see Wilson making his way toward the door. "Okay, no dilly-dallying for me today! I'm off to the children's section to make some bulletin boards. And update the social media accounts for the teen patrons! And maybe clean the breakroom!" Luna continued on as she disappeared into the stacks of the children's section.

Wilson walked up to me, nodding his head courteously at Fitz as if the cat understood the greeting. Being Fitz, however, maybe he did. The cat purred at Wilson and Wilson gave him a smile. I'd known Wilson hadn't seemed *completely* on-board when the library had first adopted Fitz, but now he was definitely sold on the orange and white cat. In fact, his attitude toward Fitz was almost as if he were a colleague and not an animal at all.

I said, "Good morning. Everything okay this morning?"

Wilson nodded absently, looking around him as if he'd misplaced something. "Where is Luna? Didn't I see her walking in with you? But I didn't see her car. Did you have to pick her up? No wonder she's so early, if that's the case."

I quickly shook my head. "No, Luna is bicycling to work now. She was here when I arrived and she said she's getting started with new bulletin boards in the children's section."

Wilson's eyebrows flew up in surprise. But he seemed eager to change the subject instead of letting me wax poetic about Luna's great work ethic and punctuality.

"I did want to talk to you about the Ask Fitz column," he said briskly.

My heart sank. Hadn't we already talked about the column yesterday? What more could possibly be said?

"Do you have a response ready for today? It might be good for Fitz to answer a question a day. I think we need to show Fitz is very responsive."

Fitz rolled over on his back and languorously stretched.

I said slowly, "I did have an answer ready for the column, yes. I've been starting out with topics that are fairly straightforward and then I figured I could move on from there. I've also been sure to list additional resources for the patrons writing in so they can find further help."

Wilson said, "Just make sure Fitz's response is all over social media."

"And the library, right?" I asked. "I figured you'd want me to print it out and put it on the bulletin board near the circulation desk."

"Well, that too, yes. But *mostly*, I want to see it on social media. That way, a lot more patrons will be able to see Fitz's advice. And then people can share the post and comment." Wilson's face, so frequently stern, suddenly became more animated. "Actually, that will be very interesting, now that I think about it. Perhaps some of the people reading Fitz's response will want to add their own advice or experiences in the comments. Or perhaps they will even disagree with Fitz's advice."

*My* advice, I thought glumly. At least I had good sources to help me give helpful tips.

"I'll be sure to share it both in the library and on social media," I said.

Wilson said, "I'm sure you will, Ann. I always have great faith in you, you know."

He was about to move toward his office when he stopped again, abruptly. "I hear a lot about video these days."

Once again, my heart sank. "Video?"

"That's right," he said brusquely. "People sharing video and watching video. The popularity of video."

"YouTube is very popular."

He nodded. "YouTube, yes. Perhaps Fitz should have video responses."

I could feel myself balking. I said lightly, "The only problem with that is we don't have a talking cat."

"Don't we?" asked Wilson. "I think we could show Fitz lolling around on the floor or chasing a toy and do a voice-over in the background. It could be another way to get more audience engagement."

I had the sinking feeling Wilson had been attending too many social media workshops at the library board meetings. "I could try to set that up," I said in an unconvincing manner.

"We have all the equipment," he said, waving his hands expansively. "I know the board would like to see it put to use, especially for projects that generate engagement."

*Engagement* certainly seemed to be the keyword here.

"This sounds as if it could be that kind of project," I agreed, sticking a smile on my face. Before he could mull this over any further, I interjected, "By the way, speaking of the board, Tanya James asked if I could run by her house around lunchtime to help her carry out some books for the Friends of the Library sale."

Wilson said, "Tanya James? Naturally! By all means, help her out. Take as much time as you need."

"Thanks," I said dryly as he hurried off. I'd figured I could count on Wilson to be very generous whenever a trustee was in need.

I glanced up as the sliding doors to the library opened and saw Burton there. He seemed to have taken special care over his appearance today and I also had a whiff of aftershave lotion, which I was pretty sure I hadn't smelled on him before. I wasn't surprised when he walked up to me and immediately asked if Luna were around.

Which is when Luna came around a corner and joined us. "Hi," she said. She still seemed completely oblivious of Burton's interest in her. In fact, she seemed to have something else on her mind entirely.

Burton said, "I was just looking for you. There's something I wanted to speak with you about."

I was about to find an excuse to make a speedy exit when I saw that Luna's face had completely drained of color. "You know," she whispered.

# Chapter Twelve

B urton frowned at Luna in confusion. "Know what?"

"I've felt so *awful*. So guilty. But I didn't want to let anyone know. I'm the only one taking care of my mom, you know. I have responsibilities. But each day, I've felt worse and worse. In some ways, it's kind of a relief to talk about it."

I said, "Luna, we have no idea what you're talking about."

Luna's head swung back and forth as she took in Burton's and my blank expressions. "Weren't you going to talk to me about the argument I had with Carmen?"

Burton shook his head. He slowly said, "No. I was going to talk with you about a possible joint project between the library and the police department."

Luna's face flushed and she covered it with her hands. "Oh, wow. I just blew it, didn't I? I guess I'd make a really bad crook."

"You sure would," I agreed. "Which is fine, since you're *not* one. Right?"

"Right. Although I've felt so terrible, like I was saying. It wasn't just the shock of discovering her, although that was bad enough. It was the fact that I'd had an argument with her and not long before she died. I feel really guilty. And I *hate* feeling guilty."

I said, "It wasn't as if you knew that something awful was going to happen to Carmen. It was just another ordinary day."

Burton took out his notebook. "Could you tell me what happened, Luna?"

She sighed and ran her fingers nervously through her purple hair as Fitz watched her with concern. "You see, it's been tough for my mother and me to make it on my salary here at the library. She's had all these medical bills, you know. I've been really trying to help make ends meet. I've been packing my lunch and everything. I'd petitioned the library board for more money at their last meeting . . . not much, just a supplementary amount," she added hurriedly. "But Carmen apparently voted against it. At least, she was the deciding vote. That's why I was so surprised, after she'd been so awesome to stand up for you, Ann."

"How did you find out that she'd voted against the raise?" I asked curiously. "That doesn't sound like something Wilson would mention."

Luna shook her head. "Nope. It was from Carmen herself. She thought it was 'impertinent' of me to ask for a raise in salary, especially since I was so new on staff. She explained the library was an *institution* and needed all the income it could get. Our jobs were to *serve*. To serve the patrons, of course, but also the library itself."

I made a face and Burton winced.

Luna said, "Anyway, I really tried to keep myself in check. I know I'm new here and I signed on to work knowing what my salary was. But I had no idea how many medical expenses my mom would have from her surgeries. And I wasn't asking for a lot. It was just the way she made me feel like I was *nothing*. Like I was being really out of line to ask for anything at all. So I admit I was sharp with her. And then I was terrified Wilson would find out."

I gave her a sympathetic look.

Burton said thoughtfully, "I didn't realize he was such a tough guy to work for."

Luna said, "He's really not. But he sure likes to butter up anyone on the library board or Friends of the Library. He wouldn't have been happy about me calling her out. But I've been feeling bad about it all. That's one reason I was coming to help bring the books up from the basement—because I wanted to apologize in person to Carmen."

Burton nodded, but looked uncomfortable, as if he'd rather Luna hadn't said anything about her argument with Carmen. I guessed this might make Luna a suspect, at least to a certain degree.

Sure enough, he reluctantly asked, "So you came up after Ann had found Carmen at the bottom of the stairs. What were you doing before that?"

Luna shifted in her seat. "I was helping a mom find a book for her beginning reader. And then I took a break and made a phone call to check on my mom." She sighed. "Too bad I wasn't giving a storytime or something like that. Being surrounded by a bunch of mothers and toddlers while I was singing, reading books, and blowing bubbles would have given me a far, far better alibi."

Burton said kindly, "I don't think anyone would consider you a very serious suspect." But I did notice he'd made a quick note in his notebook. He opened his mouth, probably to ask Luna about the joint project, but Luna was already quickly moving away. "Better run. I've got a storytime coming up."

I gave Burton a sympathetic look. "Sorry. Maybe you'll have a chance to catch up with her later? She obviously totally forgot about the project you were going to mention."

Burton smiled at me. "I'll be back." He walked slowly out of the building.

THE MORNING FLEW BY. At least it moved quickly because of a few disasters. The women's restroom had a toilet back up, a volunteer decided to shelve a cart alphabetically by title instead of author, and there was a long period of time where several computers refused to connect to the internet for a mysterious reason known only to the powers that be.

When I glanced again at my watch, I saw it wasn't only time to help Tanya James move the books, but I was going to need to really hustle to get there.

When I pulled up to her house, I was relieved to see her also just pulling up.

She smiled at me as she got out of her car. "Couldn't find anyone else to help?" she asked.

I chuckled. "I didn't even try. If you could see the morning that just transpired at the library, you'd understand."

We walked to the house and she fumbled in her purse for her keys, saying, "I completely understand. Sometimes when you walk out, you can hit the reset button on your day. I think that's why Howard likes working from home so much now."

As she started digging her keys out from the bottom of a large and very expensive purse, I said, "Tanya, it looks like your front door is already open."

She jerked her head up and frowned reprovingly at the door. It wasn't wide open, but it wasn't shut, either. "That's rather careless of Howard," she said in an irritated voice.

"He's still working at home?" I asked. I'd assumed the reason Tanya needed help lugging books was because Howard was going to be away at the time.

Her frown deepened and when she spoke again, that edge of irritation was no longer in her voice. "He's not supposed to be. That was the whole reason I asked you to help. He had a busy morning at home catching up on emails and then he was going to the office around eleven-thirty to prepare for an afternoon of meetings. Howard wasn't going to be available to help."

She pushed the door open with a forceful shove. I followed her into the atrium of the large home. Despite all the windows, the antique furniture and the gray paint and old paneling made the interior fairly dim.

On the wall, I could make out a large number of signed photographs of Howard and Tanya with various important people—political figures and celebrities, mostly. There also appeared to be several pictures with what looked like a mountain climber and well-known tennis players.

Tanya noticed my gaze and gave a self-deprecating laugh. "It looks ridiculous right here in the front of the house, doesn't it? But Howard is so proud of his connections. You know he's a self-made man? He really pulled himself up by his bootstraps and is so appreciative of where he is today."

She paused and then called out sharply, "Howard! Howard?"

Tanya paused for a moment to listen as she called, tilting her head to see if she could hear Howard upstairs. Hearing only silence, she frowned, hands on her hips.

"Maybe he's in the backyard?" I asked. It seemed like a longshot on a hot day, but it looked as though they both did some light gardening. They wouldn't have gotten the same effects from a yard service.

She listened but didn't say a word, pushing past me to head to the back door. But we went through the kitchen on the way.

I nearly ran into Tanya's back as she stopped cold. Peering around her, I could see Howard's lifeless form sprawled on the kitchen floor, a fire extinguisher on the floor beside him.

# Chapter Thirteen

Tanya was frozen in shock. After I'd quickly stepped around Tanya to make sure there was nothing we could do for Howard, I put an arm around her and helped her out of her house and to my car to wait for the police. By this time, Tanya was shivering despite the heat of the day, so I turned on my seat warmer for the passenger seat.

Burton was there within three minutes, giving us a grim nod before striding into the house to check the scene for himself. It didn't take him long before he came back out and walked in our direction.

I opened my car door to get out, but Tanya put a hand out. "Stay." She hesitated and said, "Please. I don't want to go through this official stuff without a friendly face."

I wasn't so sure my face looked at all friendly. In fact, I had the feeling it was probably stamped with the same horror I saw on Tanya's. But I nodded.

As it turned out, Burton didn't want to move Tanya, anyway. His expression was concerned and his manner, for Burton, was tentative. I couldn't really blame him. He was a new police chief and here he was working a murder of an extremely high-profile person in the town. And he certainly wouldn't want to make everything worse by approaching the mayor's wife the wrong way. In many ways, she was just as influential as her husband had been.

"I'm so sorry," he said to Tanya. "Is there anyone you'd like me to call?"

Her mouth tightened and she gave a brisk shake of her head. "No. My mother will have to know eventually, but this will be so upsetting to her. I'll have to figure out a way to break the news later." She turned finally to look at Burton and said harshly, "Who did this? Who is *doing* this? Is it the same person who killed Carmen? Don't you have any leads?"

Burton said gently, "We're getting there. Unfortunately, it can take a while for the investigation to turn up any leads. I know how frustrating that must be." He took out a small notepad and pencil. "Could you just take me through what Howard's day looked like today? I'm sorry—I know this is hard."

But Tanya had nerves of steel. She might be angry and she might be frustrated, but she was certainly not broken up about this; at least, she wasn't broken up in a way that was obvious to anyone else. She pursed her lips and said in a monotone, "It was really just like any other day, except a bit busier. Howard and I rose early and we took the dog for a walk before it became too hot outside."

Burton nodded, saying lightly, "That must have been very early."

Tanya considered this. "Yes, it was. The sun was just starting to come up, so I'm going to say it was about 6:15. That way the pavement wasn't too hot for Valentine."

Burton made note of this and then said, "What type of dog is Valentine?"

"Big," said Tanya with a short laugh. "She's a rescue, but she must have Labrador, German Shepherd, and something else big in her."

I gave her a smile. I'd seen her out walking Valentine. While the dog's name might imply she's a sweetheart, her appearance suggested she could be a force to be reckoned with.

Burton seemed to have the same question I did. "And where is Valentine now?"

For once, some emotion crossed Tanya's features and she blinked rapidly a few times before clearly becoming impatient with herself. She gave another deprecating laugh. "We tend to spoil our animals a bit. Valentine goes to the barn where I keep my horse, Fancy, stabled. They love her out there and she loves running around the property and hanging out with the horses. She even likes the barn cat there."

"And that's where she is today?" asked Burton quietly.

Tanya nodded and looked blankly out my windshield. "Howard suggested it after we walked her. Valentine seemed to want the walk to go on and on, but I was worried the pavement was already getting too hot for her paws. He told me I should drop her off at the barn for the day so she could get the rest of her energy out." She stopped and then said roughly, "If Valentine had been home, this never would have happened."

Burton gave Tanya a moment and then said, "So after you walked, you took Valentine away? And then what?"

She said, "Well, I took a shower and got ready for my day first. Then I did take her to the barn. After that, I ran a few errands."

"Grocery store?" asked Burton politely.

I wondered the same. She hadn't brought any groceries in, so it didn't seem as though that was one of the errands.

Tanya said, "We get those delivered. No, I ran by the drugstore to drop off a prescription, then I went by the dress shop. Howard had an event that was coming up and he thought I should pick up something new for it. But I didn't have any luck."

"And Howard stayed at home during these errands?" asked Burton.

Tanya shrugged. "He had work to do. Howard said he had a bunch of emails to answer and a couple of phone calls to make."

"Was that pretty much a typical morning for the mayor at home?" Burton continued making short notes in the little notebook.

"Not at all. But he'd had a very quiet last couple of weeks. We were joking about that, actually. Whenever Howard has a quiet spell, it usually means he was inundated with requests for assistance of some sort soon afterward. Sure enough, the work came barreling in. But it was also right after one of his Muffins with the Mayor. Sometimes those generate work later on. I think the events remind people they have a problem they need worked out," said Tanya.

Burton said, "So you both had an early start. Then Howard is delving into work. The plan was for him to go into the office at lunch? After lunch?"

"He'd go in after lunch every day."

Burton said, "Was this routine something people knew about?"

Tanya shrugged again. "I suppose. He hadn't been doing it for very long, but he did have a message on his voice mail at the office explaining when he'd be in every day." She paused. "Howard was already supposed to be at the office by this point. Somebody just made sure he didn't get there." Her voice was bitter.

Burton said, "I know this may be hard to think about. But was there anyone who was giving Howard a hard time? Someone who perhaps wasn't happy with him?"

Tanya cocked an eyebrow. "Are you kidding? This is *all* I'm going to be thinking about. Who could possibly have disliked Howard enough to do something like this to him?"

Burton nodded. "I know he was a likeable guy, so it might be difficult to imagine."

Tanya said, "He was a politician. Yes, he was likeable, but people didn't always think it was genuine. Besides, in his job, he couldn't tell people *yes* all the time. Sometimes people asked for his help and he either couldn't or wouldn't help them. So it wasn't as if everyone loved him all the time."

Burton waited as she thought.

Finally, Tanya said, "One person in particular stands out in my mind. Her name is Mel Trumbull. She asked Howard to vote against some zoning changes in her neighborhood. Apparently, the council is going to zone for business directly behind her house and there isn't going to be much of a tree buffer there."

Burton raised his eyebrows. "Was this woman very upset about this?"

Tanya shrugged a shoulder. "She wasn't *happy* about it. And she attended quite a few meetings about the proposed zoning changes, so she made herself practically inescapable. I was looking around me before the muffins event yesterday to make sure she wasn't lurking somewhere. I was starting to get the feeling she was going to approach us at home." She stopped short, frowning at what she'd just said.

Burton was frowning too, as he jotted down a few notes on his notepad. "Do you think that's something she might have done? Did she seem agitated?"

Tanya put her hand up to her forehead as if it was throbbing. "I don't know. I suppose she did. Her voice would get loud and squeaky when she was talking about the zoning. I have no idea what she was capable of."

Burton said, "Can you tell me a little bit about your relationship with Blake Thompson?"

Tanya blinked at him and then drawled, "Chief, what exactly are you implying?"

Burton colored a little. "Sorry, that was poorly worded. I meant your family's involvement with Blake Thompson. My understanding is he's done some work for you?"

"That's correct. But it's much more than that. Howard and I have sort of adopted him. He's practically family. He'll drop by for dinner sometimes and sometimes we'll entertain and invite him to be part of it."

"Have you always been this close to him?" asked Burton.

"No, we started out on a purely business basis. Howard was always concerned and fussing about the old wiring in the house. He seemed to think we lived in some sort of firetrap." She gave a chuckle that trembled a little bit and she stopped speaking until she regained control again.

Burton said, "So Blake has worked on some electrical issues for you, then?"

Tanya waved an impatient hand. "Electrical, plumbing, pest control, weeds in the yard. He was Howard's first line of defense with whatever problem we encountered. He even patched our roof one time."

"And they got on well, did they?" asked Burton.

Tanya snorted. "Hardly. They seemed to fight like cats and dogs. Blake would say something needed to be done that hadn't been on the agenda . . . remove mold or something. And Howard would get all red in the face and say there'd been no mention of mold or dry-rot or whatever the problem would be. Then Blake would get defensive and say sometimes you don't find out about a problem until you really get in there."

Burton nodded. "It sounds like they spent a good deal of time together."

"It's an old house. It always needs work. At least, Howard always thought it did. It's my family home. I've always lived in the house and knew things would come up from time to time that needed repairing. With Howard, it was more like he was at war with the house and determined to fix every little thing. Fortunately, we had Blake to help us out. Sometimes, he'd even try to persuade Howard that he *didn't* need to get something fixed." She gave a faint, reminiscing smile. "Howard didn't like that. He was always one for the projects. But it wasn't all work for us with Blake. He did spend so much time at the house that we started to think of him as a favorite nephew or something. We gave him extra tickets to events we attended sometimes, had him over for dinner. That sort of thing. He's a nice boy."

I didn't think he was much of a boy. And I wondered if Howard had known of Blake's relationship with Carmen. If Howard had *also* been involved with Carmen, that discovery could have made him very angry at Blake. What if Howard had picked a fight with Blake over it and then Blake had gotten mad enough to hit him with whatever was close to hand? In this case, a fire extinguisher.

Burton's mind was apparently running on a similar track. He said, "Since it sounds as if their relationship was somewhat volatile, do you think it's at all possible Blake could have done this? Maybe lost his temper for a moment?"

Tanya started slowly shaking her head. "Nooo. No, surely not. Like I said, Blake was practically family even if those two did squabble a little." But she looked less certain than she sounded.

Burton nodded and closed his notebook. "Thanks so much for being so helpful." He paused. "I'm afraid you won't be able to go into the house for a while. We have a forensics team on the way. Is there somewhere Ann, perhaps, can drive you? Someone you could visit with? Or could she bring you to the library for a while?"

Tanya gave a shaky laugh. "Well, I suppose we won't be able to collect those books for the Friends sale today after all, Ann." She considered her options. "I could go see my mother. I would just need to keep all of this from her until I can think of a way to tell her about it."

I couldn't help but wonder how isolated Tanya's mother could possibly be. After all, news traveled like wildfire in Whitby. And what about the newspaper? This was sure to be splashed all over the front page of *The Whitby Times*.

Tanya appeared to be drawing a similar conclusion. She slumped in the passenger seat. "Actually, there's no way to really keep her from hearing about Howard, is there? Not even at the retirement home. Maybe *especially* not at the retirement home with all the residents gossiping. No, I'll head over there and try to break the news gently to her. Mother was very fond of Howard."

I said quickly, "I'd be happy to drive you over there, if you'd like."

But Tanya was already decisively shaking her head. "I appreciate that, but no. I'll be all right. Plus, I think I need a few quiet moments to process this in the car before I see Mother."

After another minute, Tanya drove slowly away. Burton said to me, "Could you just take me through what you were doing here? I'm guessing it had to do with library business."

I said, "That's right—Tanya needed help transporting some of their books to the Friends of the Library book sale." I told him exactly what had happened, what I'd been doing at the library beforehand, when Tanya and I met up, and how we found Howard.

Burton nodded and rubbed his face with his hands. He groaned. "This case is going to end up biting me, I just know it. You heard Ms. James—she's already pushing for someone to be apprehended. This is one of those high-profile cases that can make you or break you."

I said, "I'm sure it's going to go just fine. Maybe if you try to treat it like an ordinary case?"

Burton sighed as two cars pulled up to join us. One of them was clearly marked as an official vehicle with the North Carolina State Bureau of Investigation. The other was a tin can of a car that made a lot of racket as it pulled up. Burton didn't seem pleased to see either one of them.

"We've got the SBI here to take care of the forensics. And we've got somebody from the local newspaper. Perfect," he said.

I looked again at the old car. Sure enough, Grayson was inside it.

"I hate to ask you this," Burton said, shifting uncomfortably on his feet, "but I've gotta, since you've now been first on the scene for two murders."

"Of course you do," I said firmly, even though my heart jumped in my mouth a little at the thought I might be considered a suspect. "Go right ahead. It's a pretty big coincidence, I know."

"How well did you know the mayor? Did you have any kind of background with him?" asked Burton, pulling out his small notebook again.

"I knew him strictly on a 'Muffins with the Mayor' basis," I said.

Burton grunted. "I need to have more 'Coffee with a Cop' events. I bet I brought in more people than the mayor did."

"Cops are always interesting," I agreed with a grin. Anyway, I wish I could be more help than that. Lately, I've pretty much spent most of my life at the library and I view everything through that lens. All I really know about him is that he was friendly, outgoing, seemed concerned about his constituents, and was usually on time showing up for the events. Although the events frequently ran *over* because he was chatting with folks."

Burton smiled. "Okay. I guess getting annoyed because events ran over isn't much of a motive for murder." He hesitated. "And Carmen? I understand you weren't crazy about her."

I smiled. "I wasn't crazy about her, for sure. But my annoyance at her attitude didn't extend so far as to make me push her down a staircase."

Burton looked relieved. "Okay, good. Good. All right, I'd better run catchup with the state police. Take care. And please don't discover any more bodies, Ann."

# Chapter Fourteen

Grayson stepped out of the car, his face lined with concern. Seeing Burton looking for a way to escape, he hurried up to him. "Is it true, then?" he asked.

That sounded like a leading question to me. Grayson likely had absolutely no idea what was going on in the James house. After all, the only people besides the state police who knew about the murder were Tanya (who might not even end up telling her own mother), and Burton and I.

"Is what true?" asked Burton, shuttering his eyes with a blank expression.

Grayson hesitated and then said, "That there's an incident here at the mayor's house. A neighbor called the paper."

Burton sighed and said, "Journalists will be the end of me. Just understand the department doesn't have an official statement to make at this time. Off-the-record, I can confirm the mayor is deceased."

Grayson's eyes were wide. "Deceased?"

"Apparently the neighbor didn't have *that* bit of information," said Burton dryly.

Burton started walking away and Grayson called after him, "Was it foul play?"

"No official statements at this time," said Burton as he continued toward the state police who were now walking inside the house wearing forensic suits.

Grayson watched him as he left. Then he slowly turned to me. I told myself to get a grip as my traitorous heart started beating just a little faster.

He said, "What's going on?"

I said, "I really shouldn't say anything either. I was here on library business and probably shouldn't make any statements, especially if Burton doesn't want to release information yet."

Grayson shook his head. "No, we're off the record here. I'm just trying to wrap my head around what's going on. Am I to understand the mayor's death was unnatural?"

I nodded. "I'm afraid so. If we're speaking off the record."

Grayson quietly processed this for a moment. Then he said, "First Carmen, now the mayor. Whitby isn't the sort of town that has a lot of homicides. Shouldn't these deaths be connected in some way?"

I hesitated. I didn't think it was up to me to disillusion Grayson if indeed he'd had any illusions about his sister.

But Grayson saw my hesitation and said wryly, "And I do know about my sister's involvement with the mayor. She wasn't any saint."

"Do you think their relationship is the reason they're both dead?" I asked slowly.

Grayson sighed. "That's what I don't know. There's also the possibility the mayor knew something about what happened to

Carmen. Maybe he had a clue as to who was responsible for her death. Then the murderer came after him to make sure he didn't tell the authorities."

My phone rang and I mumbled an apology as I pulled it out of my pocket and glanced at it. I made a face. It was Zelda.

Grayson had glimpsed the name that came up and a crooked smile crossed his face. "Oh, boy. Is she still after you to join the homeowner association board?"

"Among other things," I said, shoving the phone back into my pocket. A moment later it buzzed angrily at me as Zelda apparently left a voicemail message.

Grayson watched the chief as he walked into the mayor's house again. "I know the chief is busy, but I'd really like to talk to him to find out if he has any leads on Carmen's death. I've been planning her funeral but all I can think about is someone robbed her of all the years she had ahead of her."

I said quietly, "I can't even imagine how tough that must be. Of course you'd like more information."

He gave a harsh laugh. "The thing that really bothers me is I know whoever did this is probably going to be at her funeral."

"What makes you think that?" I asked.

He said, "Well, apparently it's someone she knew. Probably someone she knew pretty well . . . someone who wouldn't want to draw attention to themselves by *not* being at the funeral. They'd go and look sad, and all along they'd be the ones who were responsible for her being in a coffin to begin with."

His voice broke a little and he shook his head.

"I'm so sorry," I said. "I know the two of you must have been close."

"That's the funny thing . . . we really *weren't*. We had very little in common. I know some of her behavior likely led to her death. I'm not saying she was *complicit* in her own death, but that some of her behavior was bound to make people upset."

I didn't say anything, just nodded. I hoped he'd keep talking.

Fortunately, he seemed to be in the mood to get things off his chest.

"Of course Carmen was dating Elliot, but she was involved with more than a couple of men," he said, shaking his head. "I knew about Blake, but I recently found out she was involved with Howard James. I'd already argued with Carmen about her lifestyle and I didn't even realize at the time what the full picture was."

"You're thinking one of those men became jealous?" I asked.

"Exactly. That he found out about the other men and decided to tell Carmen off. Maybe it just got out of hand. Maybe he had no plans of killing her. Then, maybe, she had her back turned toward him and he couldn't resist the urge to get rid of her." He shrugged angrily.

My phone rang again and I gave Grayson a quick apology as I pulled it out to glance at it. This time it was Wilson, not Zelda.

"Hi," I said in something of a breathless voice. "Sorry, this is taking a while."

Wilson sounded a little impatient. "Did you get the books from Tanya? The library is very busy right now."

"Unfortunately, Tanya and I ran into a problem. I'll tell you about it when I get there," I said quickly. I hung up and said to Grayson, "Sorry, but I need to be getting back to work."

He smiled at me. "Of course. Sorry about holding you up."

I went straight to Wilson's small office when I got to the library and filled him in. His face went from irritated to horrified in just seconds. "Howard is dead?" he repeated. "What on earth happened?"

I hesitated. "I don't think this is for public consumption. At least, that's the impression I got from Chief Edison."

Wilson nodded his head impatiently. "Of course, of course. Why on earth would I idly gossip about the husband of a board member? I simply feel it's important for me to be apprised of all the facts."

I took a deep breath. "Absolutely. I met Tanya in front of her house and we walked inside for the books. Tanya thought it was odd the door wasn't shut."

"The door was open?" asked Wilson with alacrity. "There was a break-in of some kind?"

"Not wide open, but slightly open. Just barely pushed and unlocked. It wasn't what Tanya expected. She thought Howard was supposed to be at the office by then because he had a bunch of meetings scheduled."

"And he was inside?" Wilson shifted in his chair. He had a squeamish expression on his face.

"I'm afraid so. In the kitchen," I said.

Wilson said, "That must have been very upsetting for Tanya. And, well, for you, too. Hopefully it was quick? I'm assuming it was a heart attack or cardiac event of some kind?"

I shook my head. "No. It was murder."

His eyes opened wide. "No."

I said, "Which probably made the shock even worse for Tanya."

Wilson sighed and tilted his chair back to contemplate the ceiling. "What a mess. Maybe the library should do something as a memorial. A small plaque, maybe? Howard did a lot for the library, after all. We could rename the reading area the Howard James reading room or some such." He looked sidelong at me for a reaction.

I said, "I'm sure Tanya would appreciate the gesture."

"She was holding up all right?" asked Wilson.

"As well as could be expected. She was heading off to see her mother while the police were investigating at the house. And she was trying to decide whether or not to tell her mother what happened. Then she was concerned her mother would find out from the other residents at the home."

Wilson winced. "That's going to be hard on her. I know Tanya always handles her mother with kid gloves. I don't know if you remember, but she's brought her to library events before and has been adamant about making sure the events go *perfectly*."

"I remember," I said. I reminded Wilson that I had very vivid memories of an author tea in particular. Tanya wanted the food to be just-so. That was fine, but she also wanted it *displayed* just-so and the library was using very basic serving platters and paper plates. She insisted on bringing over her family silver, bone china, and dainty teacups for the event. I was a nervous wreck the entire time, watching people juggle the china and the teacups as they stood around and chatted. Fortunately, no china was harmed during the event.

Wilson looked as if his stomach hurt. "I also recall Tanya butting heads with Carmen during that event."

I could only imagine the stress it had caused Wilson. It had certainly made me feel uncomfortable. "That's right. It was over something small, too. Carmen wanted to go with a red, white, and blue color scheme because the author was a veteran. But Tanya felt very strongly about purple and gold because they were her mother's favorite colors."

Wilson nodded, wincing. "It's all coming back to me. As I recall, Tanya won that battle."

"Yes. I had the feeling at the time that Tanya always wanted to be in control. But then, Carmen did, too. No wonder they clashed. And that's just one example of many."

Wilson sighed and said briskly, "Well, this was a very harrowing morning for you. The best thing for you is probably to jump back into work, right? Answer another one of those Ask Fitz questions?"

"Good idea," I said dryly and headed for the office door.

The library was definitely distracting. There was a sudden swarm of mothers and preschoolers when Luna's storytime let out and it took a while to process them all because most of them had small fines for overdue books. Then there was a patron who needed help logging back into their Google account. I couldn't for the life of me figure out why Google made it so difficult to recover a password. We worked on it for the better part of an hour and then finally had some success (after she phoned a family member who she thought might possibly be a backup account).

When it was my break time, I hurried to the lounge with alacrity. I knew exactly what I was going to be doing, and it had nothing to do with *Ulysses*, despite the looming film club meeting. I was going straight to my *September* comfort read and consume some Reese's chocolate eggs that were left over from a library-hosted Easter event. Easter was a long time ago, but surely Reese's didn't go bad that quickly.

I had just settled down in the comfiest chair in the breakroom when my phone started ringing. I looked askance at it. Talking on the phone had nothing to do with my plan. Plus there was the fact I didn't recognize the phone number.

Sadly, it ended up being the mysterious number that prompted me to answer. I knew it wasn't Zelda, after all.

But when I answered the phone, it was much worse than a call from Zelda.

A squeaky voice asked, "Is this Ann?"

"Yes," I said, frowning.

"This is Kevin? Aunt Zelda gave me your phone number and said it would be all right to call you. Is this a good time?"

My heart sank. I'd seriously hoped Kevin would tell his Aunt Zelda he had no intention of being set up and to mind her own business. Now my hopes were dashed.

"Hi, Kevin," I said. "Yes, Zelda mentioned you to me. I'm at work, so I don't have very long, I'm afraid."

"How about if we go out to dinner tonight?" he said quickly, practically talking over the end of my own sentence.

My heart sank even lower. "I'm afraid it's been a pretty rough day for me today and I'm not really at my best. Are you available tomorrow? I know Zelda said you'd only be in town for a limited time."

Kevin quickly said, "Oh, I'll be here for a couple of weeks. So we have plenty of time to see each other."

"I see," I said weakly. "So tomorrow is all right? Should we do lunch?" I crossed my fingers. I only had a short lunch break. Would it be possible to confine this date to just a single hour? Surely Zelda didn't expect any more from me than that.

"Let's do dinner since we'll have more time."

Great. I said, "Sure, that sounds good. I get off at six tomorrow; will that work for you?"

Kevin sounded pleased. "Okay. Where should we meet?"

I thought quickly. There weren't many places in Whitby. Quittin' Time wasn't exactly a date-night location, but the food was always good, inexpensive, and most importantly, the service was prompt and I could leave the date quickly if I needed to. "How about Quittin' Time? It's right on the square."

"See you tomorrow at six," he said.

I hung up and sighed. My head was starting to hurt now. What was worse was that my break was nearly over. I sadly pulled out the Reese's and ate them quickly before I headed back out to the circulation desk.

I was just trying to decide whether to answer an Ask Fitz from a child who said his mom wouldn't let him have a pet or one from an adult who was having a problem with his boss at work when Blake Thompson walked up to the desk.

"Hi, Ann. I got a call from Wilson that the copier was acting up?" He gave me a broad grin, but I saw his eyes were tired. In fact, he wasn't looking as tidy and professional as he usually did.

His clothes were so wrinkled that I wondered if he'd slept in them. But then, looking at his eyes again, I wasn't sure he'd slept at all.

I said, "That qualifies as an emergency over here, believe me. It must be really bad this time or Wilson would just have asked *me* to fix it. I'll show you where it is." I left the Ask Fitz questions happily. I felt like maybe I wasn't in the right frame of mind to offer much advice about anything.

We walked up to the small room where the printer was. "Here you go." I paused. "You must be able to work on just about anything."

"No job too big or too small," he said cheerfully. "Once I'm done here, I'm heading over to the mayor's house to work on a backed up drain they've had issues with."

I winced. I knew Tanya had mentioned Blake was practically family. I hated to be the one to tell him what had happened, but it would be worse if he drove over to the house and saw all the police there.

I said slowly, "You must have been tied up with something this morning."

"Actually, I was in the next town over, doing some electrical work for a small business. Why? What did I miss?" he frowned at my serious tone.

I took a deep breath. "Why don't you have a seat?"

He shook his head. "Nope. I like to take bad news standing."

"I'm afraid the mayor has passed away," I said. It was too bad Burton wasn't here when I told Blake. I tried to make note of Blake's reactions, as I thought Burton would do if he was around.

Blake took a step backward. "No way."

I nodded. "I'm so sorry. I know that you're close with Howard and Tanya."

He was quiet for a few moments as if he was trying to wrap his head around it. "But I just saw him yesterday evening and he seemed fine."

I swallowed. "I don't think he had a natural death."

"Not natural? You mean somebody killed him?" Blake's eyes widened and he suddenly did sit down as he took this in. "What's going on here? Two murders in *Whitby*? That's crazy!" He rubbed the sides of his forehead. Then he looked up quickly, "I've got to go see Tanya. Have you heard anything about her?"

I nodded. "I was actually with her when we . . . when we found Howard. She's holding up all right, I think. She wanted to go see her mom and I thought that was probably good. That she wasn't alone."

Blake was shaking his head. He said faintly, "I just can't believe it."

I repeated, "I'm very sorry. I know Tanya said you were almost a member of the family."

He rubbed his eyes and when he spoke, his voice was gruff. "Yeah. They were good to me. I mean, they're important people in town but they always made time to talk to me like I wasn't just the guy who fixed things for them. Sometimes they host tennis players and they'd invite me over for dinner because they knew I liked to watch tennis. Used to play it in high school."

I had some vague memories of that, even though I hadn't followed the school sports much. I had the impression he'd been very good.

Blake seemed to be looking for me to say something, since we'd gone to high school together. "I remember you were a great athlete," I said quickly.

He said, "Still play tennis sometimes and try to go climbing as much as I can. I do some climbing." He looked at me sidelong, waiting for a reaction.

I made an impressed sound, although I thought rock climbing was incredibly dangerous.

"You know, I can't say I'm just totally shocked about this," said Blake in a thoughtful voice. "I mean, I *am* totally shocked, don't get me wrong. But the fact is, part of me always sort of expected some trouble. The mayor told me he'd get hate mail."

"Hate mail?" I asked, my eyes widening.

Blake hastily amended this. "Maybe more like *dislike mail*, then. Anyway, people would get upset with him for rezoning areas, widening streets, that kind of thing. He told me about it." He was quiet for a moment. "Howard could be pretty hotheaded, too. He and I occasionally got into it over stupid stuff. But we'd always make back up. Tanya was a peacemaker a lot of the time." He looked at me. "Do you think it was somebody who got upset with him with official business?"

I shook my head. "I really just don't know. I'm sure the police will be looking at all the different options. Maybe you should tell them about the letters he received."

Blake shrugged. "Maybe. But Tanya probably will." He sighed. "Now the cops are going to be investigating two crimes. I was hoping they would already have figured out who killed Carmen and put the guy behind bars." A red flush rose up from his neck. "I still think it was Elliot. Who knows, maybe the two crimes are connected. Maybe Howard happened to see something that made Elliot look guilty."

He was definitely stuck on the idea of Elliot being responsible.

Blake continued with this tantalizing possibility, "Elliot is the kind of guy who keeps his emotions all bottled up inside him until he explodes. That's what I think happened with Carmen. She told him she wanted to end things with him and he was furious. It built up inside him for a couple of hours and then he came over to the library. Maybe he thought he was just going to talk with her . . . try to reason with her, or get her to continue their relationship."

"And then his emotions got the better of him?" I asked quietly.

"Exactly!" Blake pounded his fist into his hand for emphasis. "Or maybe she rejected him again, when he was trying to persuade her to come back to him. *That* would have made him even more furious. Then he just reached out while her back was facing him and gave her a shove. It was unplanned and totally spontaneous, right? Wow, I hope he gets first degree murder and not manslaughter. Do you think he might get manslaughter?"

I didn't really want to speculate on the charges or the amount of jail time a library patron might be facing. Especially one who might be completely innocent. So instead I asked, "And you think Howard knew something?"

"Why not?" said Blake with a shrug. "If Howard knew something, Elliot wouldn't have been able to let that go. Otherwise, he'd have been living every single day wondering if the police were going to be knocking on his door any second. That's no way to live, right? He had to get rid of him."

"Did Elliot even know Howard?" I asked.

Blake laughed. "Howard knew *everybody*. Even the introverts. I'm not saying they hung out together or anything, but I bet you Howard knew Elliot. And who knows, maybe Howard had dropped by the library to see if Tanya was here and saw what happened."

"Maybe." My voice sounded doubtful to my ears.

He looked at me and gave a short laugh. "But you aren't convinced. And no wonder you aren't. Look at me. I'm a disaster right now. I can't sleep. I'm totally scattered. I'm even missing tools and can't figure out where they've gotten to."

I said, "That's totally natural. Your mind is focused on other things. No wonder you're absentminded."

One of our patrons came by, holding a stack of papers and frowning. "Hey, is the copier working yet?"

Blake muttered, "That's my cue." He turned around to start taking the copier apart while I explained to the patron that it would be just a little longer.

# Chapter Fifteen

When I got back to the desk and glanced at the clock, I realized I was going to have to scramble to set up for film club. Fortunately, I'd done most of my prep work in terms of talking about *Laura* in advance, so it was just a matter of setting up chairs, the screen, and getting the film ready to start.

While I was doing that, Timothy came in to join me. As always, he was relaxed and happy as soon as he entered the room. He was the kind of kid who was an old soul and who seemed to have a tough time fitting in among his peers. But as soon as he came into film club, he sparkled. Because he was homeschooled, his schedule was flexible enough to allow him to make it to film club and he always seemed to look forward to it.

He was sure to ask me where I was with *Ulysses*, though. I winced inwardly, thinking about the lack of progress I'd made and how I'd been running to my Rosamunde Pilcher book for a comfort read. I decided it would be better to head him off at the pass and just go ahead and fess up.

I said, "Hey, Timothy. Just wanted to let you know that I'm making some slow progress on the book. But the last few days have been crazy, so I haven't gotten as far along as I wanted. I was hoping to be able to talk to you about it today, but I'm not there yet." Nor, to be honest, even close.

Disappointment crossed his thin face and I felt awful, but then he brightened. "No problem, Ann! Actually, that will give me a chance to read it for the third time. That way I'll really have it fresh on my mind when we talk about it."

I felt relieved, even though this meant maybe I needed to be taking notes as I went. "That's perfect. Thanks, Timothy."

Another film club regular, George, came into the room. George owned a typewriter repair shop on the square that gave every indication of being very successful, although I couldn't for the life of me figure out how. He must get lots of business off the internet was the only thing I could imagine.

George clapped Timothy on the back as a greeting and Timothy grinned, even though I thought his gangly frame might topple forward from the impact. George said to Timothy, "So, we're seeing *Laura* today. Is that one you've seen? Of course, you've seen almost everything, so I don't know why I'm even asking."

I smiled. "Actually, I made a point of asking Timothy what he *hadn't* watched and picking one of those. I thought it would be more fun for him that way."

"And *Laura* is a classic," said George in an approving tone.

Timothy beamed. "Can't wait. I haven't seen a lot of noir, so this should be fun."

George settled his burly frame into a chair and said, "Ann, how are *you* doing? I read about what happened in *The Whitby Times*. Were you here working that day?"

I nodded as I fiddled with the laptop that was going to be streaming the film. "I was." I remembered the party line that Wilson was having us all say whenever we were asked about the incident. "It was a real tragedy for her family and the library, too. Of course, we've doubled down making sure the library is secure in every way." This meant Harold, our elderly security guard, had been yanked out of retirement to wander around the library every once and a while in uniform.

George listened to my spiel with a smile and then winked at Timothy who grinned back at him. "That sounds like an official statement if ever I heard one."

I laughed and admitted, "It was one. I'm not straying from it, either."

"Understood. Now another question, but this one shouldn't have a party line. How is your dating life going?"

Ordinarily, this is the kind of question that would make me bristle. But I'd known George and Timothy for a long time and this was a pretty consistent line of questioning and meant with my well-being at heart.

George continued, "You know I'm only asking because Timothy and I are living vicariously through you." He glanced at Timothy. "Unless there's a new girl on the scene I haven't heard about yet in Timothy's life."

Timothy blushed and shook his head with a shy smile. "Nope. Still just living vicariously through Ann."

I said, "As a matter of fact, I have a date of sorts tomorrow."

George laughed. "A date 'of sorts'? What kind of date is that?"

"It's a real date, but it's not one I set up for myself. And it's with someone who's only visiting in town for a few weeks," I said.

Timothy looked disappointed for me. "Doesn't sound like this relationship has much of a future."

I thought about Kevin's squeaky voice and his social awkwardness on the phone. "Indeed, it doesn't."

George glanced out the window leading into the library and raised his eyebrows. "Luna's mom is here."

Timothy said, "Good. Mona always makes really good points when we discuss the movies."

George grinned. "And she didn't even bring her knitting along this time! That's got to be a good sign."

I hid a smile. Apparently, the last film hadn't really been to Mona's liking. Maybe she knew it wasn't going to be, and that's why she'd brought what seemed to be a very large sweater along with her to work on while it went on. From time to time, she'd glanced up at the screen and given the movie a disapproving look.

I knew Luna was worried about her mom, and money, and generally everything, so it was good to see Mona looking upbeat and cheerful as she entered the room (sans knitting). She no longer had her walker, although I know Luna would have preferred she continued using it, but sported a rather snazzy-looking red cane dotted with white flowers. She also seemed to have taken some real care over her appearance, wearing a green silk top and black slacks with strands of pearls and matching earrings.

George and Timothy and I greeted her and so did the other film club members as they filed into the room behind her. Mona had a pleased smile on her face. Right now, she was basically the elder statesperson of the club and remembered seeing some of the films in the movie theater when they'd first come out. She could also sometimes provide social context as far as what was going on in the world at the time various movies came out. She was definitely a great fit for the club.

When everyone had chatted for a while and gotten a container of popcorn, I started the film. One nice thing about this group was no one ever talked or checked their phones while the movie was playing. And this particular film, from 1944, seemed to suck everyone in.

At the end, I started the discussion by asking everyone what they thought about *Laura*. Usually, at least a few of the members wouldn't have enjoyed the film. But I was glad to see everybody seemed to have enjoyed this one and had great points for the discussion.

George shook his head. "I can't imagine that guy falling in love with a dead woman. Talk about a relationship destined to go nowhere." He gave me a wink to indicate it was even worse than my doomed upcoming blind date.

Timothy said thoughtfully, "Yeah, but he was finding out more about her as he talked to people who knew her. And the more he heard, the more she grew on him. It was sort of an organic process."

I asked, "Mona, what did you think?"

She smiled. "I loved it, but I knew I would because I'd seen it before. I do remember hearing the movie was made during

World War II and they mentioned an injury the detective had sustained in a previous case a couple of times. I'm guessing that's because they had to explain to the audience why he wasn't in the service."

George said, "Makes sense. Good idea to keep the audience on the detective's side during the film."

The discussion wrapped up after another fifteen minutes and then most of the film club members spent the next few minutes catching up with each other. I spotted Luna walking by the room and give me a questioning look. She was clearly trying to look inconspicuous. I gave her a thumbs-up to indicate Mona was having fun.

A few minutes later, everyone helped me out by folding up the chairs and stacking them. Then they filed out into the library where they'd eventually make for a busy few minutes at the circulation desk because they all were readers, as well as film buffs.

I was sorry Linus hadn't made it to film club, but I wasn't surprised. It was tough for him to do anything different from his usual routine, which he followed very closely. He was also very introverted and although he might enjoy the films, he might not enjoy the camaraderie with the group as much. It was definitely something I wasn't planning on pushing him on. I was surprised to even have seen him at the Muffins with the Mayor event. Perhaps the draw had been the pastries.

Mona waited until everyone had left the room and said quietly to me, "Luna told me what happened this morning. I just hate that you had to go through that again. What on earth is going on? Do the police think the crimes are connected, or is Whitby suddenly this really dangerous place?"

I could see worry etching lines into her face. "No, I don't think the police think these deaths are random at all and I don't think you should be worried about your safety. Chief Burton is working hard on it and I know he's going to find out soon who's responsible."

Mona was still fretting a little. "I feel so bad for Tanya, too, having to find Howard like that. She has always been such an overprotective person; she must hate that she had no way to keep this from happening. I remember one time I was taking a walk. These were in healthier days," she added wryly. "Anyway, I remembered there was something I wanted to ask the mayor about. Just a minor thing about the town's garbage collection services. Tanya answered the door and was *such* a gatekeeper. She told me Howard was busy doing other things and I needed to make an appointment at his office."

I made a face. "Ouch. She wouldn't even let Howard speak for himself?"

Mona laughed. "Of course, she was right. The mayor wouldn't get anything done at all if people were dropping by his house and office all day. But it still stung. That's just an example of how much she looked out for him. I can't even imagine what she must be going through now. And she seems to be the same way with her mother, too." She glanced up and spotted Luna peering in the window for just a second before spotting her mom and hurrying away.

It was so comical that I had to really work hard to keep a smile from pulling at my lips. Mona gave me a rueful look and then started chuckling and then we were both laughing. "Speaking of overprotective," said Mona, "I think Luna needs to chill out a little."

I said lightly, "Well, she's just looking out for you."

"As long as she's not looking out for me *too* much. There are things I'm interested in doing," said Mona with a smile.

I was glad to see she was being so outgoing. I remembered a time when Luna had to work hard to get Mona to even leave her house. I said, "You have some fun plans?"

"They'd *hopefully* be fun. I'm wanting to date. Oh, you know, nothing serious. I was just thinking that it would be fun to have a companion to do things with. It doesn't have to be the romance of the century or anything. But from time to time, it would be nice to head off to the movies or a restaurant with someone. I might even be up for a light stroll and a picnic as long as the walk wasn't too steep."

"Do you have any prospects?" I asked, trying not to be pushy. But she had come to the library looking a lot more dressed-up than I usually saw her. "Or do you already have some dates planned?"

"I don't have anything planned, yet," said Mona. She paused and added quickly, "What do you know about the older gentleman I always see here in the library?"

"The older gentleman?" I asked. There were quite a few regulars. I was hoping she was talking about one of the other regulars and not Linus. Linus was such an introvert and seemed so dedicated to the memory of his late-wife that I wasn't sure if he could be drawn-out at all. I hadn't even been able to convince him to make it to film club. I couldn't imagine him asking someone out on a date.

"Yes, the one who's here in a suit every day. He always seems to follow a particular routine where he starts with the newspapers and then moves on to books." She flushed. "He's a nice-looking older man."

She was definitely talking about Linus. I didn't want to raise her hopes, but I definitely didn't want to discourage her, either. Who knew? Maybe Linus would be receptive to having a friend to do things with. Who was I to stand in the way? I said cautiously, "I think you're talking about Linus. He's very nice." I hesitated. "And he's very quiet. For years, he never really said anything more than *good morning* to me."

Mona tilted her head to one side. "But he's more outgoing now?"

I said, "I wouldn't call him outgoing, but he is speaking a little more, although he still follows his same schedule every day. He's a real creature of habit. Luna was actually the one who was able to get him to open up a little."

Mona gave a fond smile. "Yes. Yes, she's good at that. Sometimes she's a bit pushy, but she loves to talk to people."

"Let me know how it goes," I said, giving her a small hug.

After I finished cleaning up after film club, I sat back down at the circulation desk and enjoyed the fact that the library had suddenly become very quiet. I took another look at the Ask Fitz questions.

*Dear Fitz,*

*I don't know what to do. Sometimes I can't control my temper. I did something bad—real bad—to a woman I cared about. Now I've panicked and done something bad again. I'm feeling a little crazy and I don't know what I might do next. Help.*

*Signed,*
*One Hammer Short of a Toolbox*

# Chapter Sixteen

I stared at the email. It couldn't be, could it? Was this a confession in the guise of someone seeking help? I read it through again. Maybe all I could think about right now were the murders, but it seemed like the person who wrote the email had done something serious. To me, with the mention of 'losing my temper,' it didn't sound like the person was talking about cheating on a girlfriend.

And so I called Burton right away. And he *arrived* right away. We walked into the breakroom to make sure we weren't overheard.

He grimly read the email a few times and then sighed and rubbed his face with his large hands.

I said hesitantly, "I didn't want to make a mountain out of a molehill, but I figured this was something you'd want to know about." I clicked on the email's header to see if I could find out any information on the sender. Then I snorted in disbelief.

Burton leaned in closer and snorted, too. The email appeared to be sent from the library's own server. The email was sent from inside the library.

"Do me a favor and don't respond to this one," he said in a wry voice.

"Of course not. Do you think there's something in it? Could it possibly be the person behind Carmen's and Howard's deaths?" I asked.

He said, "I really don't know. But it's a lead and I'm taking it seriously." He paused. "This signature makes it sound like Blake Thompson could be involved."

I was already shaking my head. "I just don't see it. He'd have to be stupid to implicate himself. And he's not a stupid guy."

"Now I know you went to high school with him and all, Ann. But you have to agree this looks a little suspicious. At least answer me this: has Blake Thompson been in the library lately?"

I made a face. He'd just been in fixing the copier, of course. He could have easily used an app to set the email to send later, after he'd left the premises. Then I remembered something else.

"Yes," I said reluctantly. "He was here recently. And he did mention to me that he was missing some tools."

Burton nodded and stood up. "Thanks so much for calling this to my attention, Ann."

I watched as he walked out the breakroom door.

Later at the circulation desk, I struggled to focus, still thinking about Blake and unable to shake my conviction that he had nothing to do with the email that was sent to me. I finally got back into the Ask Fitz emails, glanced through them, and (not finding anything else alarming in the inbox), picked a question to answer.

Since this was Fitz the cat responding, I figured I would keep things from being too dark. I carefully wrote out Fitz's advice, along with a photo of Fitz looking sympathetically into the camera. Like the others, I signed it Your Friend, Fitz.

I read it through a few times, tweaking a few things, and then emailed it over to Wilson to see if it fit his vision for the column, as I had for the previous ones.

I saw he'd emailed back immediately. "Post it!" was all the email said. So I quickly did.

Luna came by right as I was hitting send. "How's it going?" she asked. "Holding up okay?"

"I'm going to be sleeping well tonight." I rubbed my eyes.

"At least you don't have your date tonight, right?" asked Luna a mischievous glint in her eye.

"Well, I didn't want to fall asleep at the table in front of the poor guy," I said lightly. "Although part of me wants to go ahead and knock it out. Dates have a way of hanging over me."

Luna shook her head. "You're way too keyed up about romance. You should just set out on a mission to enjoy yourself! Have some food, some conversation, maybe a glass of wine. Look at it as a break from the ordinary."

I sighed. "Apparently, I'm not that well-adjusted. It's always pretty stressful for me." I hesitated. I wanted to talk with someone about the email we'd received and Burton hadn't told me not to share it with anyone . . . only not to respond to it.

"Here's something else that's stressful," I said. I pulled up the email and showed it to Luna.

Her eyes grew wide as she read it. "Oh, wow," she breathed. "I know."

Luna said, "Wait. Did you show this to the cops?"

"I sure did. But I don't really feel good about it."

Luna glanced over the email again. "Because it so obviously points to Blake?"

"Exactly. I mean, he's not stupid enough to *do* something like that. He wouldn't have signed an email that way, you know? I feel like somebody's trying to set him up. And the email was sent from the library. I checked."

Luna gave a low whistle. "What did Burton say?"

"He's checking it out, of course. He has to. I just hope Blake doesn't get locked up over this. To me, it's basically a fake confession letter." I put a hand up to my forehead where it was starting to pound.

Luna opened a drawer behind the desk and pulled out a couple of aspirin for me. I took them from her as she casually asked, "On a completely separate topic, have you noticed anything different about my mom?"

I hesitated. I wasn't sure if Mona would want me to tell Luna that she was setting her cap for Linus. I wasn't even sure she *was* setting her cap for him—it just might be she was simply interested in finding out more, since he was so inscrutable. "Different?"

"Yes. She seems really outgoing today, for one. I mean, don't get me wrong, I'm glad she is. I was so worried about her when she didn't even want to leave the house. Plus, she's all gussied up today for some reason. A silk blouse for a day at the library?"

I said, "Maybe she was excited about going to film club and she was just looking for an excuse to look nice. I know sometimes getting dressed up makes me feel better," I said.

This was actually a blatant lie. Whenever I felt under-the-weather or down in the dumps, I felt way better when I put on yoga pants and a baggy tee shirt and curled up with Fitz and a good book on my sofa.

Luna seemed to sense the lie but wasn't totally ready to call me out on it. "Really?" She looked at me through narrowed eyes.

"Sure." I was eager to move off the subject of Mona's sudden desire to dress up for a trip to the library. "By the way, your mom seemed so engaged at film club today."

"No knitting this time?" asked Luna with a smile tugging at her lips.

"None at all. And she was able to fill in a little background information for us for the time the movie was made."

Luna said, "She's still getting along well with everyone in the group?" Her voice was doubtful as if she couldn't really picture her mother hanging out with a teenage film buff and a type-writer repairman, among others.

"Oh, she's definitely one of the gang."

Luna opened her mouth as if she was going to ask more questions, but then stared across at the door. "Uh oh. Looks like Mel is here and she doesn't look happy."

I followed her gaze and saw that was an understatement. Mel looked like she hadn't slept in days. There were dark circles under her eyes, and her clothes were rumpled and stained with what appeared to be coffee. She spotted us and started hurrying in our direction.

"At least it's quiet in the library right now," said Luna.

Mel came right up to the circulation desk and leaned against it as if she needed some support. "I'm so glad you're both here," she said, her eyes wide.

"What's happened?" asked Luna breathlessly. She seemed to be steeling herself for more bad news.

Mel's bloodshot eyes filled with tears. "Oh, I heard about the mayor. It's so awful."

I was a little surprised Mel would be so upset about the mayor's death. Although it was a small town and everyone knew everyone else, I'd heard that, if anything, Mel had been on the outs with the mayor because of the zoning issue near her house.

Mel continued with a hiccupping breath. "And it's not just that. I haven't been able to sleep since Carmen died. I feel terrible about it."

Luna shook her head and said in a firm voice, "You have nothing to feel terrible about. Friends squabble sometimes—you know that. You had absolutely no idea Carmen was going to die before you two had an opportunity to make up. Why would you? She was a healthy young woman."

Fitz came bounding up at this point. I swear the furry boy has some sort of built-in radar to tell him when someone was upset. He slid across the smooth surface of the circulation desk and peered with great concern at Mel with his large, green eyes. She reached out a hand for him with a muffled sob and he bumped his head against her as a few tears trickled down her pale cheeks.

The interaction seemed to help Mel pull herself together a little. She continued rubbing Fitz as she said quietly, "You're right. I had no idea Carmen was going to die. But I still shouldn't have fallen out with her. It really wasn't any of my business what she was doing with the mayor. And now the mayor is dead, too."

Luna glanced over at me helplessly.

I said gently, "Mel, their deaths were tragedies. But you didn't have anything to do with them. You shouldn't feel guilty."

Mel looked unconvinced. "Thanks. I'm trying not to, but it's really hard. Carmen and I were *friends*. I feel like I ran out on her when she needed me the most. I should have been there for her. Instead, I wasn't even talking to her. Maybe she would have told me something was going on. Maybe there was someone who was giving her a hard time. Then at least we'd know who might have killed her." Her voice trembled over the last few words.

Luna reached out a hand and rubbed her arm. Her voice was kind as she said, "The police are working hard to find out who did it. I'm sure they'll arrest someone soon."

Mel buried her face in Fitz's fur for a moment. In a muffled voice she said, "I think they already have."

"*What*?" Luna and I chorused together.

Mel gave us a miserable look. She quietly said, "On the way over, I saw Burton walking Blake into the police station."

I suddenly felt as if I couldn't breathe. I finally stammered out, "In handcuffs?"

Mel quickly shook her head. "No. But it didn't look friendly. I'm really worried about him."

I said stoutly, "Mel, Burton is probably just having a conversation with Blake. There's no need to read anything else into it than that."

"I know you're right. It's just that I'm such a nervous wreck over all this violence. And I feel so bad about the mayor's death ..." She paused and then said, "I'm worried, too." Her voice dropped to a whisper. "I was there this morning."

I felt myself grow very still. "There? At the mayor's house?"

She nodded and closed her eyes briefly. "I was on my way to work and kept thinking about Carmen and how awful I felt about how I left things with her. My anger. My harsh words. You probably don't know about this Ann, but Luna does; I've been having an ongoing fight with town hall over zoning near my house. Anyway, the last town hall meeting, I got really upset. Nobody seemed to really be listening to me. I blew up."

Luna said stoutly, "I don't think that *blew up* really describes what happened, Mel. You were just frustrated, that's all. And you had a right to be. It's your house. The last thing you want when you go home at night is to have a lot of noise and lights from a restaurant behind you when you're finally trying to relax for the day."

Mel gave her a grateful look. "That's true. But I didn't handle it the right way at all. I was so upset and I yelled at the mayor and said all kinds of things I didn't really mean. Anyway, this morning, I was thinking about that and about Carmen. I decided to run by his house on the way to work and apologize for what I said and the tone of voice I used. I mean, he's a professional and he was doing what he thought was right for the town. I just took it all too personally."

Luna said quickly, "That was a very nice thing to do."

"I just felt bad about the whole thing. I think the reason I got so upset wasn't just because of the zoning change. It was also because of his relationship with Carmen. I felt that made a statement about him and the kind of person he was," said Mel.

I nodded. "In a way, it did."

Mel said, "It did. He was the kind of person who'd cheat on his wife with someone a lot younger. But again—that wasn't any of my business. Anyway, I ran by his house. It was pretty early, but I knew he and Tanya were early morning people because I've seen them out walking their dog before I head to work."

I asked, "Did he come to the door? Or Tanya?"

Mel shook her head. "No. Tanya's car wasn't even there, but his was. I was wondering this morning if maybe he was trying to avoid me, which I totally understand. But what if he was already *dead* then?" She gave us a horrified look. "Or maybe he wasn't even dead, but he needed help? What if whoever killed him was inside? And I just walked away?"

Luna said forcefully, "Mel, remember, you had *nothing* to do with his death. The only person who did is the person who murdered him."

Mel said miserably in a very quiet voice, "And now I'm scared to tell the police I was there. I mean, they're going to think I *did* do it, even though they seem like they're interested in Blake right now."

"They won't think you did it," said Luna soothingly. "There has to be evidence."

Mel said, "But there's motive. I was arguing with both Carmen and the mayor before they died. And then I was at the scene of the crime."

I pointed out, "You don't really know if you were there at the time of the crime. It could be the mayor was in the shower and didn't hear the door. Or maybe you're right and he peeked out the window, saw you, and didn't feel like answering the door because he didn't know what you were going to say."

Mel considered this, a spark of hope in her eyes. "Do you really think so?"

"We don't know exactly when he was murdered," I said. "I don't think you should worry about not being able to help him. After all, if he *had* been in there with the murderer when you arrived and you confronted him, you might have been his next victim."

Mel gave a small shiver.

I said, "Was there anything else you noticed while you were there? You said Tanya's car wasn't at the house."

Mel considered this for a moment. "Well, I saw Blake leaving. He didn't see me, though," she added quickly. "He looked like he was leaving in a hurry. I know from when he was dating Carmen that he always had a lot of jobs to work and lots of last-minute jobs. I just figured he was late heading out of there." She looked at us with big eyes. "You don't think Blake had anything to do with the mayor's death, do you?"

"Do you?" asked Luna.

Mel shook her head, alarmed. "No, of course not! I mean, I couldn't believe it when I saw Burton and Blake going into the police station. I even sent him a text before I came here asking him what was going on. Blake and Howard always got along so great with each other. Well, I guess sometimes they had little spats, but it was always over silly stuff and they made up right away. Blake was always going over to the mayor's house to have dinner with them or to see a movie or something."

Luna knit her eyebrows. "Now, that's something I wouldn't have expected. I mean, there's a big age difference between Blake and Tanya and Howard James. Plus, there's a big difference in their backgrounds."

Mel frowned. "You mean because Blake is blue-collar? I guess so. Carmen told me Blake was like the son they wished they had. He seems like he can do anything . . . he's just one of those really, really capable people. He knows how to fix plumbing stuff and electrical problems. I got the impression that they admire him because he's so handy and can do all the stuff they *can't* do." Mel dropped to a quieter voice, as if not wanting to be overheard. "And they weren't able to have children of their own. Blake has filled that spot in a lot of ways. It's not just that he can do anything workwise, he's also so athletic and has so many hobbies and interests."

It sounded like Mel had a bit of a crush on Blake. Her voice, when she spoke of him, was awed.

Mel continued, "I've always really liked Blake and he was always friendly to me when the three of us were hanging out. Sometimes we'd go out to dinner together and Blake never made me feel like a third wheel. And I see him a lot because I work at a paint store and Blake does some painting on the side." She blushed. "Like I said, he can do anything. And I just know he didn't have anything to do with Howard's death. He just wouldn't have it in him."

Her phone pinged and Mel eagerly looked at it. Her face lit up. "It's him! Blake, I mean. The police released him."

Luna and I grinned back at her. "That's great news," I said.

Mel looked at her watch and said reluctantly, "I need to be going." She smiled shyly at Luna and me. "Thanks so much to both of you. You've made me feel so much better. I guess I really just needed to talk it all through. I've had all these thoughts bottled together in my head for so long and I just don't know what to make of them. You've helped me sort them out. Maybe I can actually sleep tonight for once."

Mel gave Fitz a farewell rub and buried her face in his fur once more. "And thanks to you, too, Fitz."

We watched as Mel left. Luna gave a low whistle. "I really like Mel, but boy, she's an emotional wreck right now."

I said, "At least she seems a little better than she did when she came in."

Luna said, "Yeah, but she had nowhere to go but up." She paused and then looked at me. "What did you think about her ardent defense of Blake? I mean, she saw him at Howard's house this morning."

"I think she's likes Blake. Maybe she has a crush on him, too."

Luna nodded. "That's exactly what I thought. And she's determined to cover up for him. Well, I can't let that pass. I know it's hearsay, but I'm going to let the chief know the next time I see him. Then Burton can tell Blake he was spotted there the morning Howard died and ask him why he lied about it." She squinted across the library at the clock. "Oops. I've got to get ready for storytime." She hurried off.

I was worried about something else, although I didn't want to share it with Luna. Luna was Mel's friend and fiercely loyal to everyone she cared about. But I kept thinking about Mel as I tickled Fitz under his chin. She clearly had warm feelings for him. She wasn't in a relationship and I wasn't sure when the last time she *had* been in a relationship was. It could be her love life was as messy as mine was. Mel had argued with Carmen about Carmen's relationship with the mayor . . . someone who Blake considered a father figure. What if Mel had struck out at Carmen in frustration?

And what if the mayor had seen something? Mel had already admitted being at his house and was already upset with Howard because of the zoning issue. Could Mel be more dangerous than she seemed?

# Chapter Seventeen

The rest of the day was fairly uneventful, which allowed me to get books shelved, some research completed, and some routine tasks done. I had to lock up the library that night and had to really hold onto my patience since there were a couple of patrons who didn't seem to want to leave. When I finally got back home, I was determined to get through at least a couple of episodes of *Ulysses*. Afterward, I fell into a deep sleep and was startled by my alarm going off the next morning. I often woke up just a few minutes before my alarm made a peep. This time I was so surprised to wake up to its beeping that I was fully awake in seconds.

When I got to the library, Wilson was just pulling into the parking lot. Luna was pedaling furiously up to the building in order to be walking in where Wilson could witness her punctuality. I could spot Fitz in one of the library windows, looking amused and taking it all in.

Wilson hopped out of the car, clad in his usual suit and holding his briefcase. He greeted both Luna and me (Luna gave him a rather breathless greeting in return) and then said, "Ann, we have an interlibrary loan request that came in yesterday. I was wondering if you could personally handle it this morning."

I looked curiously at him. Usually an interlibrary loan was given a few days to process and was handled by the county. I said, "Sure, I'd be happy to take care of it."

My reply must have sounded more like a question because Wilson said, "It was a board member's request so I thought we could expedite it, that's all. Thanks. I'll delete it out of the system then. It's a book the college has. I'll jot down the information for you."

Now I was a little more interested. If I was at Whitby College, maybe I'd have the chance to glimpse Elliot in the parking lot or walking across campus.

Less than an hour later, I arrived at the college campus. Instead of parking directly outside of the library, I parked behind another academic building in the hopes of having a better opportunity to run into Elliot.

I was mulling over Blake's intense anti-Elliot feelings when I heard a voice calling out to me.

"Hey. Ann?"

I turned around and saw Elliot. Wow. I had no idea it would be *that* easy.

"Hi, Elliot. On your way to class?"

He was carrying a backpack and a couple of books. He shook his head. "Just on my way to my office. It's upstairs at the library. Listen, I just wanted to let you know you can't park where you did unless you have a parking pass. The school is awful about towing cars. It would be safer to park over at the library." He gestured to the building. "I'm guessing that's why you're here, anyway. Business at the library."

I was chagrined. Now I was going to miss my opportunity to speak with Elliot because I'd be moving my car. "Oops. Thanks for the tip. The last thing I need is to pay to get my car back."

I hurried over and quickly moved my car. I moved it *so* quickly in fact, Elliot was just walking up to the library when I hopped out of my car.

He gave me a smile. "You should be fine there."

I smiled back at him. And hesitated. Now that he and I were speaking, I had absolutely no idea how to broach the topics I wanted to talk about. I could hardly ask him why Blake was so determined to throw him under the bus for both Carmen's and the mayor's death. And I couldn't just come right out and ask him where he was yesterday morning when the mayor was murdered.

Fortunately, Elliot spoke, probably to fill the gap in conversation that was starting to feel awkward. "How are you doing?" he asked in a kinder voice. "I know it must have been rough finding Carmen that way. Has life gotten more back to normal for you?"

I realized then with a good deal of surprise that Elliot clearly didn't know about the mayor's death. But then, college campuses provided a sort of bubble that protected you from the rest of the world. Or could he possibly be just pretending he hadn't heard, as a cover? I said slowly, "Unfortunately, not. You've probably been busy on campus and haven't heard."

"Busy? When?"

I said, "Yesterday morning."

He shrugged. "Depending on the time, I was either teaching or in my office at the library."

I took a deep breath. "I was with Tanya James when we found her husband."

Elliot stopped short then, brows knitted. "*Found* him? What do you mean?"

"He'd been murdered at his home," I said in a quiet voice.

Elliot looked absolutely stunned. He was either hearing this information for the first time or he was a marvelous actor. "No," he breathed. He glanced quickly at his watch. "Here, I have a few minutes."

He directed me over to a long bench near a fountain.

I started over. "I was meeting Tanya to help carry some books from their home to the library for the Friends of the Library used book sale. When we got there, the door was unlocked, which made Tanya concerned. Howard was already supposed to be at the office, apparently, because he had meetings. He didn't answer when she called him. Then we found Howard in the kitchen." I didn't want to go into the cause of death since Burton seemed to not want to go into details when he was speaking to Grayson.

"And they're sure it wasn't a natural death?" asked Elliot, even though I'd already mentioned murder.

I nodded.

Elliot sat there for a few moments, staring blindly at the fountain. He said, "I can't believe it. Two back-to-back murders in Whitby. What's going on?" He gave a harsh laugh. "This is really difficult for me to take in. I'm still having a tough time processing Carmen's death. And I'm not even family! I can't imagine how hard this must be on Grayson, losing his sister this way. But I can't help it—I've been absolutely devastated by her death."

I sat there quietly with him for a bit.

He finally turned to me and said, "If you found Howard yesterday, you must also have spoken with the police."

I nodded. "Mostly just to tell the chief what had happened and why I was there."

Elliot said, "Did you find out if they had any updates? If they're following any leads? Whoever is doing this is still obviously on the loose. They might even kill again."

I said, "I'm sure the police are doing everything they can to find out who's behind these deaths. But I didn't find out any news from them, no."

Elliot sighed. Then he said slowly, "Carmen was just so full of life. It's hard to believe she's gone." He glanced at me again. "You might have had a different impression, knowing Carmen on a professional basis."

I answered cautiously, "I didn't really know her well since I only was acquainted with Carmen through work. But I always found her very organized and efficient. Every event she put together was always extremely successful."

Elliot gave an absent nod of his head. "It might be hard to believe, but Carmen was the kind of person who brought people together."

I thought this might be a bit of a stretch, but I nodded amiably. From what I'd witnessed, Carmen could also be very divisive when she wanted to be.

I said, "It sounds as if she was a good friend, herself. I know she and Mel had been friends for a while."

I hoped he would either contradict me or add something. Elliot did.

He said, "She was. Although Carmen wasn't perfect. She and Mel were having some sort of spat when Carmen died. But you know how that is . . . friends sometimes don't get along all that well."

He paused. "Like I said, Carmen wasn't perfect. And she was the most complicated person I knew. Maybe that's one of the things that attracted me to her—she was a puzzle for me to try and figure out."

I nodded and Elliot continued.

"Sometimes I couldn't really understand where she was coming from. Her relationship with Blake Thompson, for one." He considered this for a moment and then said, "Actually, I think I do understand it, at least on a certain level. Blake probably seemed refreshing for someone like Carmen. He isn't complicated like she was. What you see is what you get with him and she probably liked that. There's absolutely no subterfuge there." He sighed. "And now there's no point trying to figure out Carmen anymore. She'll forever be a mystery."

I said slowly, "Going back to the mayor, I was wondering if anybody had any public feuds with him. Or old grudges." Elliot looked at me curiously and I gave a self-deprecating laugh. "I guess I feel somewhat invested now. I'd like to see whoever did that to him brought to justice."

Elliot considered this in a sort of bemused, professorial way. "I suppose the spouse is always technically the prime suspect.

Although you said Tanya was with you, didn't you? When you found the mayor?"

I nodded. "That's right."

Elliot said, "I have a tough time picturing Tanya as much of a killer, though. She's far too blue-blooded." He glanced at his watch and said reluctantly, "I should head up to my office and finish preparing for my upcoming class. Thanks so much for taking the time to fill me in; I know you were here on library business."

As he hurried away, I couldn't help but think of Blake's reaction to him. Elliot may think Tanya didn't look like a killer, but I thought Elliot seemed even less like one.

Back at the library, it was business as usual. At least, it was until my phone rang. I was surprised to hear Tanya James on the other end. As usual, she sounded very composed. But there was a note of urgency in her voice, too.

"Ann? Hi. I hope you're having a more normal day today," said Tanya dryly. There was a note of strain in her voice.

I said cautiously, "How are you doing, Tanya? Is there anything I can do for you?"

"Actually, there is. I left so quickly yesterday morning I felt I didn't really even have a chance to speak with you about . . . what happened."

I said, "And let me just say again how sorry I am about Howard."

Tanya said quickly, "Thank you. Yes, it's been very hard, not just for me but for my mother. At this point in her life, I'm really trying to keep everything *pleasant* for her. I feel like she should just live out the rest of her years peacefully, without any real troubles or grief."

This sounded like the impossible dream to me. Wouldn't Tanya's mom experience grief at the loss of her friends? Wouldn't she have challenging days as well as good ones? Out loud I said, "Of course. I completely understand that. How did she take the news?"

There was a pause on the other end of the line and then Tanya said, "I gave her a slightly alternate version of events. I told her Howard had passed away, but didn't tell her it was a violent death. I honestly didn't see the purpose in upsetting her."

"I see." Although, again, I thought it might be difficult to protect Tanya's mom from this information for very long.

Tanya sighed. "Honestly, it was still very upsetting for her. Her vision is very poor so she doesn't read the newspapers anymore and I've spoken with her friends at the home and asked them not to divulge any details about his death. I was hoping perhaps you could keep some of the gorier details of Howard's death to yourself? It would be very helpful if you didn't speak with the press. I got the impression the police chief isn't planning on releasing any information yet, either."

"I won't say a word about how he died to the newspaper," I said.

Tanya's voice was a bit lighter now. "Thank you. I really appreciate it." She paused again. "I'm so sorry for calling you at work. I hope I'm not keeping you."

"Oh no, it's actually fairly quiet here now," I said.

She said, "It's just been very difficult for me to believe this could happen. I must still be in a state of shock. There was one other thing I wanted to ask you. Do you know Elliot Parker at all? I believe he visits the library a good deal."

"I do know him, as a regular patron of the library. Sometimes he'll come in to work or read for a while."

Tanya said, "It's just that he had this tremendous argument with Howard a few days ago."

"An argument?"

Tanya said, "That's right. I was just coming home from running errands and Elliot was inside with Howard. I couldn't really hear what they were saying. Technically, I suppose, it was Elliot ranting instead of an actual *argument*, which assumes two participants. I didn't hear Howard speaking at all."

"Did they have any business with each other?" I frowned. "I mean, Elliot works at the university, so I wouldn't think they'd have business in regard to Elliot's work. But maybe there was something he needed from the mayor's office or the town hall? Could it have been town business?"

Tanya seemed to be weighing this on the other end. Then she said, "I don't know. It simply didn't sound like business to me; it sounded personal. But the house is big and the walls are thick and I couldn't make out what he was saying."

I paused. "You could call Elliot and ask."

She gave a short laugh. "I did. He immediately brushed me off and got off the phone as quickly as possible."

I asked, "Are you planning on telling the police about it?"

Tanya sighed. "I really feel like I should. It actually feels wrong *not* to tell them about it because it seems like the kind of information they'd want to know about. But at the same time, I'm torn—I don't want to get Elliot into serious hot water when there might be no reason to do so. What's your impression of him? Does he seem to have a hot temper?"

I couldn't really think of any reason why Elliot would have displayed a loss of temper in the library to begin with. If someone took too long at the copier machine? If someone took his seat while he was getting another book out? I said, "No, I've never seen him lose his temper. Although I'm not sure there would have been much cause to at the library."

"No, of course not." Tanya sounded disappointed. "Well, I've taken up too much of your time. Hope you have a good rest of your day, Ann."

# Chapter Eighteen

B ut the rest of the day wasn't shaping up to be all that great. After I finished at the library, I hurried to the staff restroom really quickly to freshen up before my dinner with Kevin. I smoothed down my hair and took a paper towel to wipe away a mysterious stain from my lunch that had somehow migrated to my sleeve. Then I applied a smudge of lipstick. It would have to do. I muttered Zelda's name under my breath as I headed out the door.

It seemed to be a quiet night at Quittin' Time, which suited me well. As the hostess greeted me at the door, I said, "I'm actually supposed to be meeting someone here. Is there anyone already here waiting for another party?"

The restaurant hostess gave me an apologetic look and shook her head. I stifled a sigh and said, "Could I wait at a table?"

Ten minutes later, there was still no sign of Kevin. I checked my phone for the tenth time and didn't see any messages. Should I call him? Text? Leave? How long should I wait before I took off?

I felt bad about taking a table, especially as the restaurant was filling up. I went ahead and ordered a glass of wine and sent Kevin a quick text. *Just checking in*, it said.

A deep voice that decidedly wasn't Kevin's squeaky one said, "Hi, Ann."

I looked up and saw Grayson standing there.

"Oh hi," I said in a somewhat breathless voice that definitely didn't sound like mine. "Good to see you."

"I was just catching something to eat real quickly after leaving the office." His eyes were tired, but he gave me a warm grin that made my heart beat faster. "Do you mind if I sit with you?"

I hesitated. It was exactly what I wanted. What I'd always hoped would sort of accidentally happen so I didn't have to make the first move. Anyway, he was just being friendly . . . it didn't look as if he was searching for any sort of romantic interlude. At the same time, though, was I being stood up? Or not?

I ended up saying reluctantly, "I would really love that, but I'm actually supposed to be meeting someone here. I'm not sure if he's running late or if I'm being stood up." I gave a short laugh.

Grayson backed up a step and looked apologetic. "I'm sorry. I shouldn't have assumed you were eating alone."

"Oh no, that's *fine*. Absolutely fine. I usually am. The evening is honestly something I'm not really looking forward to," I said, wanting to explain about Zelda and the nephew and the blind date. But that was exactly when a squeaky voice said, "Ann?"

I glanced up and then stood up as a very tall 30-something with thick glasses and a pocket full of pens stood in front of my table. He looked at me and then he looked at Grayson.

Grayson quickly held out his hand and introduced himself. Then he said to me, "Good talking to you, Ann. See you later."

I watched miserably as he walked away to an empty table across the room and then I forced a smile and greeted Kevin. He sat down at the table with me and immediately started reading the menu.

I glanced at my watch. He'd been almost thirty minutes late. Shouldn't he at least apologize? But he'd already moved on to the food he was going to eat and started peppering me with questions about what was good at the restaurant.

"Are the buffalo wings spicy?" he asked, pushing his glasses farther up his nose.

I said, "For buffalo wings, you mean? They're definitely spicy, but I don't know they're all *that* strong. I'd ask the waitress when she comes around."

But he'd moved on to other entrees with a frown. "Is the shrimp and grits any good?"

This continued until the waitress came by the table. She asked if we were ready to order and I gazed helplessly at Kevin. I'd known what I wanted before I even arrived at the restaurant, but Kevin seemed like he might ponder his selection for a while.

He didn't answer and so the waitress asked, "Need a few minutes?"

Kevin again didn't answer, so I did. "Yes, please."

The waitress ended up coming back by two more times and each time Kevin didn't even look up from the menu. The third time, I prompted him, worried we were going to be at Quittin' Time all night. Plus, by this time, I really *was* getting hungry. Lunch had been a long time ago. "Kevin," I said desperately, "are you trying to decide between a few different things? Maybe our waitress can help you decide."

This finally made him look briefly up from the menu. "I have four possibilities."

He listed them and the waitress gave a brief summary of the various popularities of the dishes with customers and the best points of all of them. Then she hesitantly made a recommendation.

Kevin, still seriously considering all of them as if his selection was a life or death decision, carefully said, "Then I'll get the pork chops. But could you leave the onions off?"

The waitress made a note on her order pad. "Of course."

"And could you put the gravy on the side?"

"I'll definitely get them to do that." She made another note.

He gave her a few more changes to the dish before she hurried off to the kitchen to put the order in. Unfortunately, I saw a large party of what seemed to be an entire office had already submitted their order and it appeared to be heading to the kitchen before ours.

I stifled a sigh and smiled at Kevin. Now the excruciating ordering process was over, maybe I could find out a little more about him. "Kevin, your aunt didn't really have an opportunity to tell me much about you. Could you fill me in?"

His eyes lit up behind his thick glasses as if it was a question he didn't often hear. Then he launched into an exhaustive narrative about himself, giving no opportunity for me to break in. He started with his birth, listed all the teachers he'd had in school through the years, talked about his favorite foods and things he hated, then launched into his career in information technology and the tasks he completed on a daily basis.

He was just starting to talk about the different organizations he belonged to in high school when the food arrived. I stifled yet another sigh as the waitress cheerily put down the two plates. Kevin regarded his with suspicion.

To cover my discomfort at the way he was picking his food up with his fork and studying it, I started a halting, brief narrative of my own. Kevin, however, wasn't listening. He finally took an experimental bite of his food and made a face. "The gravy is sort of spicy. And I don't think the meat is done the way I want."

Before I could respond, he'd waved over the waitress. "This isn't very good," he said.

I blinked. Usually, if you sent something back to the kitchen, you'd ask them to make a change somehow. Not just tell them it wasn't good.

The waitress, I have to say, was excellent. She seemed sympathetic, made eye contact, and nodded. Then she said, "I'm so sorry and I totally understand. Can I offer you a gift certificate for your next visit with us?"

Kevin's mouth pulled down in a frown. "I'm really just passing through town. I don't live here."

Thank goodness.

The waitress said, "May I at least bring you a free dessert? On the house?"

Kevin looked up at the ceiling and paused for a moment as if to build tension for his response. I was already thinking of ways to wrap this date up as early as possible. A sudden headache? Something I forgot to take care of at the library?

Kevin finally answered, "Well, all right. I suppose that will have to do. Could you bring me a dessert menu?"

The waitress did and Kevin said, "I'll need a few minutes."

I felt my blood pressure rise as he again carefully studied the short dessert menu, talking about his dislike for coconut and the way chocolate sauce was rarely made well.

I started to tell him I was really going to need to cut the evening short when he waved the waitress over and peppered her with questions about his top three choices.

At this point, I reflected again on the fact I needed to stop getting set up for blind dates, period. I'd never had one go well or that had led anywhere. Usually, the only reason I went on them was out of a sense of obligation to the person who was trying to set us up.

Finally, Kevin reluctantly placed his order, as if sure he'd made a terrible mistake somehow. I wasn't sure how you could go wrong with chocolate cake and ice cream, but he seemed convinced it was very possible.

He glanced across the restaurant and then reached out his hand and held mine. I was so shocked my first instinct was to shrink away from him . . . which I did. I followed his gaze and caught Grayson's eyes before he colored slightly and looked away, apparently thinking he'd interrupted some sort of intimate moment.

I was just about fed up by this point. I gave Kevin a tight smile and was about to tell him I'd had a long day and really needed to head out when his phone rang. It was a ringtone that was some sort of rap music and I flushed as other diners looked our way. I watched as he slowly realized the ringing was coming from his own pocket and then even more slowly pulled the phone out.

"Aunt Zelda?" he asked into the phone.

He listened for a few moments and then said, "Okay. I'll be over in a minute."

Kevin raised his hand and called the waitress over. "Do you have the dessert ready? I have to go."

The waitress hurried back to the kitchen to get the dessert packaged in a to-go container.

I said, "Is everything all right? Is Zelda okay?" Not that I wanted this horrid date to continue, but it did seem very abrupt.

He shrugged. "She just needs some help with her phone, that's all. She figured supper was about over."

He stood up and glanced over at Grayson's table again, but he'd mercifully left. "Good to meet you," he muttered as the waitress returned with the to-go container.

As he left, I realized he'd left me to pay the entire bill.

I was finally walking out of the restaurant a few minutes later, feeling like I just wanted to crawl into the bed. I heard my name and turned to see Elliot coming into the restaurant. He had a slight smile on his face.

"Long time no see." He chuckled. "We seem to keep running into each other."

I smiled back at him. "Having a dinner out?"

He said, "Just take-out. I do that about one night out of the week. Ordinarily, I cook for myself and then freeze part of what I make for later."

I said, "I've been meaning to do that, too. I can't ever seem to remember when I'm at the store to get the *full* recipe amount.

I think I've been on my own so long, I just automatically halve everything. But I'd save myself so much time if I froze half of what I made."

Elliot said, "It's good to do. But then I do get really sick of my own cooking and that's why I like to grab take-out. It's kind of my reward for cooking and eating healthy the rest of the week."

I laughed. "Are you saying Quittin' Time doesn't have healthy menu options?"

He grinned. "About the closest they come to healthy is the Italian salad. And it's loaded with cured meats."

"Very true." As I got to know Elliot a little better, he seemed a lot more approachable than he sometimes had in the library. He was always *friendly* in the library, but seemed very academic and remote. Now I could see more what Carmen had found attractive about him. But the thought of Carmen made me think about the two murders again. Which made me think about the fact Tanya had just told me her husband and Elliot had argued before the mayor's sudden death.

A shadow must have fallen across my features because Elliot frowned. "Hey, what's wrong? Is something on your mind?"

I hesitated. There wasn't really a good way to bring this up politely, so I just blurted it out. "You know how small towns are with people talking. I overheard something today." I figured that sounded better than the fact I was listening directly to gossip. "Someone was saying they'd seen you arguing with the mayor."

Elliot's eyes shuttered. "I see."

"I'm sorry. I thought you should know."

He said, "No, I'm glad you told me. I wouldn't want the first time I heard about it to be from the police. And the way gossip travels in this town, I'm sure the police will be hearing about it soon." He sighed and glanced around him quickly to make sure our conversation was still private. "Yes, I did have an argument with Howard. I hate to think about it now because he's gone. That's one of the lessons in all of this—make sure you make up with people before too much time goes by. You just never know."

I waited, hoping he'd fill me in on the argument.

Elliot said, "Actually, I've been wanting to get it off my chest. It makes me feel guilty that we argued. I mentioned to you earlier Carmen wasn't exactly an angel. She had lots of different relationships and *most* of the time, I wasn't under the illusion I was the only person she was involved with."

I nodded in an encouraging way.

He sighed. "Like I said, I could understand the attraction somebody like Blake had for her. But then I saw Carmen and Howard together."

I winced. "Where were you?"

He said, "I was in Asheville recently for a weekend away. That's when I spotted the two of them together."

I asked, "Together, as in having a conversation?"

"Together as in having a relationship," said Elliot with a distasteful expression. He sighed. "The thing was, I'd known for a while I didn't have any claims on Carmen. She'd made it more than clear she wasn't interested in an exclusive relationship with me. Or, actually, with anybody. But seeing her with the mayor was something different."

I said, "Maybe you should give the police chief a call. I'm sure it's the kind of information he'd probably find useful."

Elliot shook his head quickly. "I'm not sure it means anything. It's just a connection. Carmen had plenty of connections." He gave a harsh laugh.

I said, "So you went over to confront Howard about it."

"For the second time." He gave another short laugh. "The first time was before Carmen died. To me, it was all Howard's fault. After all, he was a lot older than she was. He had a lot of life experience. He was *married*. He should have been the responsible party. Maybe part of me also just wanted to mess up Howard's relationship with his wife like I felt he'd messed up mine with Carmen. I thought maybe his wife should know what had happened."

"Did you talk to Tanya?" I asked.

He shook his head. "I didn't have to. I'm sure Tanya overheard. She showed up right as I was letting Howard have it. I didn't mean for her to learn about it like that." He looked down, grimly. "Then Carmen and I argued about it when I saw her at the restaurant. That's mainly what we were discussing—her relationship with Howard. I just couldn't accept she could do something so underhanded. Not only was she hiding the affair from Blake and me, she was encroaching on a marriage. Plus, Blake regarded Howard as a father figure—it was incredibly inappropriate for Carmen to pursue the mayor."

I said, "And then you confronted Howard about it again? Before he died?"

Elliot bobbed his head. "I wasn't thinking straight. At first, I wasn't going to say anything. But after Carmen died, part of me wondered if Howard could have had something to do with her death. Maybe Carmen threatened to speak with his wife about it if he didn't divorce Tanya and marry her."

My eyes opened wider. "Is that what you think happened?"

"I just don't know. It's a possibility, though, isn't it? Anyway, the more I thought about it, the more I was convinced Howard could have done it. But here he is . . . murdered, himself."

Elliot suddenly looked tired. "Look, I should go grab my take-out. I'm pretty exhausted and ready to call this day done."

"Of course," I said quickly. "Good seeing you, Elliot."

He lifted a hand in farewell and strode into the restaurant.

# Chapter Nineteen

The next morning, I walked into the library first. Fitz greeted me right as I walked in, which was exactly what I needed. I'd have taken Fitz home with me last night if I hadn't had that date. I sighed as I thought of it and vowed once again to tell everyone I was allergic to blind dates.

Fitz seemed to understand I was tense and immediately curled up in my lap when I sat down at the circulation desk to do some work. I rubbed him absently as I booted up the computer and felt some of the tension melting away as I did. Maybe I needed to write him an 'Ask Fitz' letter. He certainly was good at helping solve my problems.

I checked in on the response to his latest column and saw it had been shared a lot and on different social media platforms. I guessed that had something more to do with the adorable picture of Fitz accompanying the piece and less with my fairly pedestrian advice and the list of helpful references I'd highlighted.

A few minutes later, Luna and Wilson had arrived and shortly afterward, the rest of the staff. I suddenly realized today was the biweekly staff meeting. As the secretary for the meeting,

I was in charge of the minutes. I quickly rifled through my purse and, relieved, found my digital voice recorder. It made creating the minutes so much easier.

The meeting ended shortly before the library opened to the public and covered a lot of different topics, including holiday staff schedules, access to digital textbooks, and a new feature Wilson wanted to try: Patron of the Month.

I switched off the voice recorder and was about to file out of the community room with the other staff members when Wilson stopped me.

"Carmen's funeral service is today," he said briskly.

"This afternoon, isn't it?" I asked. "We're all working, though, of course."

Wilson said, "It's at noon, actually, so during lunch. I think it's important for the library to be represented there. We always need to employ prudence when dealing with library board members. They're our advocates. Besides, Carmen was an instrumental part of our programs and passed away on the premises. I think a couple of representatives would be best. You and I can go."

"Sounds good," I said. I looked down at what I'd worn to work. "Do I look all right for a funeral?"

Wilson peered at me through his glasses as if actually seeing me for the first time. "That's a rather jaunty top, isn't it?"

I'd thought the same thing. My black slacks were fine, but when I was getting dressed this morning, I'd eschewed my usual neutral top for something a little livelier, since I'd felt the need to cheer myself up a little. "Will it do, or do you think I should run home and change?"

Wilson glanced at the clock. "Why don't you run back home and put on something a little more somber-looking? It's fairly quiet here now, since we've just opened." He gave me a nod and walked briskly away to his office.

I motioned to Luna and told her what Wilson had said. "Can you cover the circulation desk if things suddenly get busy? I should be right back."

"Sure," she said. Then she said, "I'm sorry to ask you to do one more thing, but do you think you could stop by my mom's house and pick her up? I didn't get a chance to talk to her this morning before I biked off to work, and I forgot she wanted to hang out here today."

"No problem," I said. "Could you call her and let her know I'll be there in just a few minutes?"

Luna nodded and then made a face. "I think she has a project for you later, too. She wants you to help her create a profile on this online dating site."

I raised my eyebrows and chuckled. "I'm not sure I'm the one who should help anyone try and procure dates. I'll have to tell you about my disaster last night."

Luna said, "I knew anyone related to Zelda wasn't going to work out. But, getting my mom's profile shouldn't be bad. She wants you to take a picture of her and help her write her bio and stuff. I offered to help, but she acted horrified when I suggested it. Apparently, she thinks I'll come up with something really wacky. As if!" Luna tossed her newly-pink hair. She must have dyed it last night.

I smiled. "I'll try to come up with something good."

Thirty minutes later, I was back at the library with Luna's mom in tow and wearing a suitably solemn blouse. I was relieved to see the library was still quiet because Mona was ready to set up the profile.

"Do I look all right?" she asked, patting her snowy white hair.

"You look perfect," I said honestly. And she did. She was wearing a bright blue top that set off her hair perfectly. Mona had artfully applied makeup that accentuated her eyes. "What do you want to use as a background for your profile picture?"

She glanced around and said, "I'll just stand in front of one of the bookcases. After all, if somebody isn't interested in books, it's not going to work." She peered across the library and asked, "Is Linus here?" She snorted. "Never mind. I know he's *always* here."

I hadn't wanted to ask, but the fact that she was setting up a dating profile made me think things hadn't gone especially well with Linus. "He's here, yes." I hesitated. "How did everything go on that front, by the way?"

Mona rolled her eyes. "He was perfectly polite. He carefully answered every small talk question I sent his way. But he clearly didn't want the conversation to actually go anywhere because his answers were super short."

She seemed to be looking for some reassurance from me and I quickly gave it. "I wouldn't take it personally. That's the way he always is. I still have really short conversations with him and some days Linus doesn't seem to want to talk at all. He'll just give me a smile or a quick wave and that's the end of it. He's just very quiet and private."

Mona said, "Well, I don't want to wait for him to loosen up. And it makes me feel weird to be the only one trying to make conversation. That's why I thought the online dating might work out. Have you tried it?"

I shook my head. "I'm still hoping for serendipity. But it's hard to come by in a small town."

Mona snorted. "Tell me about it! Try serendipity when you're my age." Her brow wrinkled for a moment. "You do think there are men my age using online dating apps, don't you?"

"Let's try it and find out," I said with a smile and we spent the next fifteen minutes getting her all set up.

The rest of the morning flew by and the library went from fairly quiet to extremely busy. Luna had a couple of storytimes and the kids and their moms all found loads of books to check out. I had a patron interested in finding out more about how to research genealogy. Aside from that, the copier went on the blink again.

Before I knew it, Wilson was at the circulation desk and telling me it was time to head out for Carmen's funeral. I smoothed my hair down with one hand and grabbed my purse from underneath the desk in the hopes of fishing out my lipstick and reapplying it.

The drive to the cemetery was a short one. But by the time Wilson and I arrived there, there was already a crowd of people. Wilson muttered, "I should have realized we needed to leave earlier. Carmen was too high-profile not to have a large number of people attending her funeral service."

I glanced at my watch. "We're still early. And we can speak with Carmen's brother after the service to make sure he realizes we made it here." I ignored the way my heart made a silly flutter at the thought of Grayson. Grayson, who probably was still under the delusion I was dating Kevin. I grimaced.

The service was simple but meaningful. There was a soloist who gave a lovely rendition of "Amazing Grace" and Grayson gave a wonderful eulogy for his sister. I had the feeling that Grayson had been able to see a different side to his sister; a side not many people had the chance to see. But then, Carmen was also being mourned by Blake and Elliot, both of whom were in attendance.

Blake, actually, was in terrible shape. His face was pale and sweaty. From time to time his shoulders shook with silent sobs. I hoped the service would give him some sense of closure and the chance to heal.

Elliot was clearly a less emotional person—at least in the most obvious of ways. But I could see the tension in his back and shoulders as he sat ramrod straight in the folding chair. He blinked rapidly once as if to force back any tears that might be imminent.

Thirty minutes later, the service was over. Wilson started heading over to the receiving line where Grayson stood. I walked a few steps with him before he shook his head. "I think it looks better if we're not together. I'll go ahead and wait in the line and then you can speak with him nearer the end."

I nodded, sighing inwardly. Wilson could be very particular about appearances. I sat on a concrete bench to wait for my turn to stand in the receiving line.

While I was sitting, Blake came toward me, apparently heading for the parking lot. He staggered, stepping wrong on a slight incline. I stood up and took his arm. "Here, Blake, have a seat for a minute."

He turned and gave me a grateful look, still half-blinded by tears. "Thanks, Ann."

We sat there for a few minutes quietly while he regained control. He gave a final, shuddering sob and said in a more-normal voice, "Thanks again, Ann. Geez, what a week. Sorry. I don't usually fall apart like this."

I said, "You don't have anything to apologize for. I totally understand."

He gave me a smile. "I figured you would. You're a librarian, after all. You're good at listening to people."

"Just give yourself time, Blake. After a tragedy like this, it takes time to heal." I thought about my aunt and my mother and all the losses I'd had. To this day, I still feel saddened thinking of them and they were years ago.

Blake rubbed his eyes and said gruffly, "Yeah. That's what I think it's going to take—time."

He looked over at Tanya, waiting quietly in the receiving line to speak to Grayson. I saw Wilson still wasn't halfway up the line yet, so I had a little bit of time.

Blake gestured to Tanya. "Then there are people like Tanya. She just lost her husband and she's cool as a cucumber. And I've been a wreck. Maybe it's just the fact there were two deaths so close together or something." He glanced over at me. "And I'm worried about the cops thinking I'm involved in this stuff. I figure you know since you work at the library but in case you don't, Burton questioned me down at the station for a while. Somebody's trying to set me up."

I said in a low voice, "I do know about it and it didn't ring true for me at all. There's something else you should know, though. I've known you for a long time, Blake, and want to make sure you know someone saw you over at the mayor's house."

He blanched. "What? You mean yesterday morning?"

"That's right. They mentioned it to me when I was talking to them. And if this person mentioned it to me, they probably said something to Burton, too."

Blake dropped his head into his hands and moaned. "This just gets worse and worse."

"What happened?" I asked him gently. "Do you have a reasonable explanation for what you were doing there? Maybe you can tell the police and get in front of the story instead of having to be defensive about why you were there."

Blake raised his head and gazed seriously at me. "It's not the best of explanations."

"But it's the truth, right?"

He gave a short laugh. "It's the truth, but it isn't something that's going to make me look less guilty. Plus, if word gets out, it could really affect my business. I *have* to be trustworthy. People hire me to be in their homes, sometimes when they're not even there. If people think I might be dangerous, they'll just hire somebody else to do contract work in their house."

I said, "Like I said, maybe it's not as bad as it seems. Why *were* you there?"

He sighed. "I'd spoken to Elliot." He gave another unhappy laugh. "Maybe *spoken* isn't the right word. Maybe it's more like *yelled at.*"

"When was this?"

Blake said, "It was the evening before the mayor's death. Elliot actually called me on the phone. I could tell he'd been drinking and he sounded really agitated. Not like him at all. You know how he's always sort of cool and collected."

"Remote," I said.

"Sure, that's a good word for it. Anyway, he wasn't the other night. He sounded totally worked up. I think he was crying some, too."

I asked, "Why did he call?"

Blake said harshly, "Because he wanted to make me as unhappy as he was. He wanted to share the misery. He'd apparently seen Carmen with the mayor before Carmen died. I didn't want to even believe it. I called Elliot all kinds of names. Howard knew I was dating Carmen. He *knew* it. I couldn't believe he'd do something like that to me. And I couldn't really believe *Carmen* would do something like that to me. That she'd betray me like that. Somehow it hurt much worse than her being with Elliot."

"Because Carmen knew you and Howard were close."

"Right," said Blake. "It's like she totally betrayed me and I couldn't even ask her *why* because she's gone."

"So you went over to talk to Howard."

Blake snorted. "Talk? I was going to let him have it. I couldn't ask Carmen what she'd been thinking and so Howard was the only one I could ask about it."

"What about Tanya?" I asked.

Blake said, "I wasn't really even thinking straight, but I figured she should probably hear about it, if she was around. I mean, I'd stewed about it all night. Like I said, at first I didn't want to believe it. When I got off the phone with Elliot, I poured myself a drink and tried to settle down. Then I ended up pouring myself another. Then a few more. I even ended up calling Elliot back and screaming at him for phoning me in the first place. But he'd been drinking so much by then that I don't think it even registered. Then I finally realized the guy was telling me the truth, not trying to just mess with my head. That's why *he* was so upset. That's why *he* was drinking so much."

"That's when you decided to confront Howard."

"Right. When I finally believed it, myself. So I was over at Howard's house in between jobs. It's amazing I even was able to concentrate on the first job while I was thinking what I was going to say to Howard."

"Did you see him? Howard, I mean?" I asked, feeling myself tense as I waited for his response.

He shook his head. "Nope. I banged on the door and rang the doorbell and even shouted at the door like an idiot a couple of times, thinking maybe he was just trying to avoid me because he knew why I was there." He shook his head again, this time sadly. "It really hurt me, you know? To think he would do something like that to me. I mean, I looked at Howard as a father figure. We were close."

"So he never came to the door and you left."

"Exactly. But now somebody has seen me there. I'll guess I'll have to tell the cops about it, but it sure doesn't look good." He brightened. "Elliot was just as upset as I was. And he was totally wasted on the phone. Maybe *he* went by there and murdered Howard." The idea was clearly appealing to him.

I glanced over at the receiving line and saw Wilson had just spoken with Grayson and was looking my way. "I'd better run speak with Grayson before he leaves."

He nodded, now clearly distracted thinking about Elliot and his potential involvement in Howard's death. "See you later, Ann. And thanks for being an ear."

Grayson looked exhausted; his eyes were red with emotion. He shook my proffered hand and thanked me for coming, although he seemed a little reserved—whether from the solemn occasion itself or our awkward run-in with Kevin, I wasn't sure.

When Wilson and I got back to the library, things were definitely not quiet anymore. Apparently, most of the town of Whitby had descended on the library. Luna was checking out books and gave me a frantic expression. There was a water main break nearby and no water was running, which meant none of the toilets would flush. Wilson jumped in to help check out patrons while I hurried over to the computer room where several of the computers had some sort of login issue. Then two new volunteers arrived for first-day training. The phone was ringing off the hook for some reason. And several unsupervised kids in the children's area were playing tag.

After about twenty minutes of total mayhem, we finally managed to get things under control. It was then the phone started ringing again. I stifled a sigh and said, "Whitby Public Library."

"Ann?" asked a patrician voice.

# Chapter Twenty

I briefly closed my eyes. It was Tanya. And I had a feeling I knew what she was calling about. "Yes, this is Ann."

"It's Tanya James. I'm sorry to bother you; I know you've had a busy day. I meant to try to talk to you at Carmen's funeral, but I was caught up in a conversation when you were leaving."

"It's no problem at all, Tanya. What can I help you with?" I figured I should figure out her reason for calling before the library was descended upon again.

She said briskly, "It's the books for the Friends of the Library sale again. The forensics investigation is all finished now. I see the books and they're making me sad when I look at them." Her voice was hard as if she was angry anything could make her feel that way. "It's silly. It's simply because we were on our way to send them to the library sale when we found Howard. Regardless of how silly it is, I'd like them out of the house. Now."

The library began buzzing with activity again, right on cue. But I knew Wilson would rather pitch in himself than have Tanya James upset no one from the library was giving her a hand. "Of course, Tanya. I totally understand. I'll let Wilson know and run right over there."

"Thank you for understanding," she said rather stiffly before hanging up.

I hurried back to Wilson's office, tapping briefly on the door before letting myself in.

He gave me a weary look. "What now? It really can't get any worse, can it? Jonathan just went home sick, so now we're down another librarian."

I grimaced. "Bad timing. The library is getting really busy again. Plus, Tanya James called me and wants me to run over there and collect those books."

"Now?" Wilson blinked.

"Yes. She said that looking at the books is reminding her of Howard. She asked if I could go right over."

Wilson made a shooing motion with both hands. "Then go right over! I'll hop out there on the desk for a while. And maybe those volunteers can jump in and help out."

I winced. The volunteers had experienced a very rushed training with me and I wasn't even sure they'd remember how to do any of the things I showed them. But I nodded and rushed out of the office to my car.

A few minutes later, I pulled my car up into Tanya's driveway and as close to the house as I could. I wasn't sure how many books Tanya was talking about, but I wanted to make sure the task was as easy as possible.

I knocked on the door and Tanya immediately answered, a cool smile on her face. "Thanks again for this, Ann."

I smiled back at her. "Happy to help."

She led me inside and helped me carry a few bags of books to the car. She snapped her fingers. "You know, there are a few more from upstairs I could donate. If you'll wait for me a minute, I'll throw them into a bag and you can take those, as well."

I followed her inside and waited downstairs while she gathered the books from somewhere upstairs. Their dog, Valentine, nuzzled me and I absently stroked him while I glanced over their collection of signed photos in the downstairs hallway. There was one in particular that kept drawing my interest and I wasn't sure why. I studied it carefully. It was a sort of photo montage of a climber on top of a craggy mountain and the bottom photo was of Tanya, Blake, Howard, and the climber here at the house over dinner. The climber had signed both photos. All of them were grinning toothy grins.

I was startled when I heard Tanya's voice behind me and calling my name, now even a bit chillier than earlier. I jumped a little and turned around, automatically holding out my arms for the bag of books Tanya was clutching. She looked displeased or disappointed, as if I'd been snooping somehow. But, after all, surely the photos had been placed on the wall to show off how many famous and interesting people the couple knew.

She carefully handed it over. "Here you are, Ann. I promise this is the last time I'll recruit you for this."

I smiled at her. "I hope that doesn't mean you won't be buying any more books."

Tanya smiled back, a bit warmer this time. "Actually, I think it *does* mean that I won't be buying more books. At least, I won't be buying printed copies. I'm making the switch to ebooks. And I'll be supplementing my reading with books from the library. So I'll be seeing you there, I'm sure. I won't keep you any longer—thanks again."

When I returned to the library, it was just as busy there as it had been earlier. It wasn't until I took my break that I realized how much my feet hurt. I slipped off my shoes for a few minutes in the breakroom and gave a sigh of relief. I glanced up as Luna popped in.

"Just needed to grab my juice from the fridge. I've started juicing again," she said. "Kale, beets, carrots, celery, cucumber. Trying to be healthy." She removed a rather scary-looking brew from the fridge.

"Is it good?" I asked doubtfully.

"Good *for* you," said Luna. Her gold tooth glinted as she gave a big grin. She stooped to rub Fitz, who'd followed me into the lounge. "Maybe a little love from Fitz will be good for me, too."

She paused, then continued in a deliberately offhanded way as she nonchalantly stroked Fitz under his chin, "Say, what do you know about Wilson?"

I frowned, confused by the question. "Not much. He doesn't exactly share a lot of personal information."

"Has he ever been married, or anything?" she asked innocently.

Now I stared at her. "Are you . . . you're interested in Wilson?" I blinked at her. I supposed that Wilson wasn't all that much older than she was, although he frequently seemed it because of his manner, his stiff decorum, and the formal way he dressed.

Luna stared at me, her eyes huge. Then she burst out laughing. "Me? And Wilson? Only on a desert island. Or maybe during the zombie apocalypse."

I felt somewhat relieved at this. I couldn't imagine the two of them together. "Well, they say opposites attract," I offered weakly.

"Not to *that* degree," said Luna with a snort. "So, *was* he married?"

I shook my head. "He had a longstanding relationship with one woman, but then she moved away for work. I guess Wilson must not have felt moved to marry her and the relationship broke off."

Luna looked around and said in a low voice, "You've got to keep this under wraps. Mom might be interested in Wilson."

I was nearly as surprised as when I'd thought Luna was interested in Wilson. "Really?"

Luna chuckled. "Yep. I was shocked, too. I mean, he's a lot younger than she is. I guess he's probably exactly in between my age and Mom's. Anyway, she was just asking a lot of questions about him and I couldn't answer them. So thanks."

I guess Mona had given up on Linus. It was probably a good thing, since I had the feeling Linus was still in love with his deceased wife and wasn't quite ready to move on yet. I didn't want Mona getting hurt. But I also wasn't sure Wilson was the best choice for Mona or anybody. He seemed married to the library to me.

The library remained busy the rest of the day and the day was a complete blur by the end. I had to close up that night, too, so I was the last one there. I made a tired sweep of the library, finding one patron asleep in an armchair near the quiet section. It took a few minutes for him to wake up enough to gather his things and leave . . . and then he decided to visit the men's room before leaving.

I made sure Fitz was settled in for the night with some fresh food and water and gave him a rub before heading out the door and locking up.

I felt at this point as if I was running on autopilot as I got into my car. There was one last car in the parking lot that started up after I did and I sighed. Must be the sleepy patron trying to give himself a minute to be more alert before he drove back home.

I drove up to my house and parked the car, thinking over my supper options in the house. None of them sounded good but neither did going out to a restaurant and spending money. I fished my keys out of my purse and decided I'd just heat up some frozen meatballs and add it to the leftover pasta I had. That would make my leftovers a little more interesting.

I fumbled with my keys before getting to my door and dropped them somewhere on the brick walkway leading up to the little house. It was already dark outside and I peered at the ground, trying to spot them.

That's when I heard an icy voice behind me and then heard the jingle of my keys as a hand swept down to retrieve them.

"I was hoping I'd find you here, Hi, Ann."

# Chapter Twenty-One

I froze and then tried to study Tanya's face in the darkness. Was this some sort of library business visit? My gut told me it was something very different, but it also wouldn't be good if I made a mistake and accused a library board member of something nefarious.

I gave a shaky laugh. "Oh, it's you, Tanya. You startled me." Something in her expression and the way she held my keys made me reach slowly back into my purse and switch on my digital voice recorder I'd had handy for the library meeting this morning.

Some of my ambivalence must have translated to her because her eyes narrowed. Suddenly, I thought back to earlier in the day and the photos on the wall of her entrance hall. The climbing photo with the autograph and the smiling faces in the bottom photo. Then I thought about the Friends of the Library sale: the very reason I was at Tanya's house today. Which made me think of the rest of the books for the sale in the library basement, and Carmen at the bottom of the stairs.

Tanya said smoothly, "I haven't been able to sleep well since Howard's death. We had so many years of being together that I suppose it's the break in the routine that's making it all so hard. So I've taken to exercising at night before turning in. I was walking down your street and saw your car. Cute house."

I tried to keep my voice steady. "Thanks. It was my aunt's house, which explains why the garden is so nice." Of course, it was too dark for Tanya to even see the garden. I hurried on, "I'd invite you in to see it, but the truth is today was pretty crazy at the library and I'm going to fall right into bed as soon as I eat." My voice cracked at the end of the sentence.

Tanya said, "I'll only be a minute." And she jabbed something that felt like a gun into my stomach.

With shaking hands, I unlocked the front door and opened it.

"We're going to talk about why you're so nervous," said Tanya in a remote voice. I saw that what she had wasn't a gun, but a hammer.

"Maybe because you forced your way into my house and are clutching a hammer for some reason," I said in a frosty voice of my own. It had been a long day. And now one of our library board members appeared to be a killer.

"I think it's more than that. I think you know something," said Tanya.

"Know something? Yes. But until you got heavy-handed with me, I hadn't put it all together. Thanks for the help," I said. "Let's catalog what I know. I know you found out about Carmen's and your husband's affair when Elliot was yelling at Howard about it."

Tanya's eyes narrowed. "Apparently, it was less of a secret than I thought."

"I know you were supposed to be at the library the morning Carmen died but 'didn't show up.' I know that was unusual behavior for you."

Tanya shrugged.

"So I know you *were* actually there to help Carmen with the Friends of the Library sale," I said. I took a deep breath. "I know you must have been very angry with Carmen. You seem as though you've always had a good relationship with Howard and I've never heard any rumors about him straying before."

"Because he didn't," Tanya enunciated.

"I know you must have confronted Carmen about it. Not only would you have been angry on Howard's behalf, you would also have been angry on Blake's. After all, Blake has always been like a son to you. He has meals at your house, he's invited over when you have special guests. You wouldn't have been happy to know his girlfriend was cheating on him—especially with your husband," I said.

Tanya didn't say anything this time.

I continued, "I also know Carmen wasn't the kind of person who did well with criticism of any kind. She had an argument with a coworker of mine who was upset about not getting a small raise because she thought that my coworker was blaming her. Carmen wouldn't have let your accusations pass without firing back."

Tanya's color rose at the memory. "As if she had a leg to stand on. She was completely immoral."

"I know she turned her back on you to continue down the stairs. And I know you must have been carrying something heavy and hit her over the head with it. When Carmen fell down the stairs and was motionless, you must have taken your leave before anyone saw you. Then we would all think you were either running late for volunteering or that you simply couldn't make it after all."

Tanya studied me coolly. "This is all just speculation. There's nothing the police could use to convict me."

I continued, "Let's see what else I know. I know Howard must have figured out that you were responsible for Carmen's death. You must have confronted him about the affair and it came out in the resulting argument. Because of *course* you would have argued about it with him. There was no way you'd have allowed his infidelity to get a free pass from you."

Tanya was quiet again.

I said, "You argued. It got heated. You reached out for the weapon closest to hand in the kitchen, which was the fire extinguisher. And Howard went down. The only question is whether you'd *planned* on eliminating Howard. Was it your pride? You knew you already had a convenient way of discovering his body because you and I were going to pick up the books for the sale. Maybe you decided to pick a fight with Howard to kill him and then discover him with me tagging along."

Tanya muttered again, "Complete speculation. Nonsense."

"If it's such nonsense, why are you holding a hammer? Why are you at my house after dark?" I asked. "Let me answer for you. It's because of my trip over to your home today, isn't it? You called me to pick up the rest of the books. Maybe when you looked at them, instead of feeling sad, like you'd told me, they made you feel guilty, instead. Regardless, you wanted them out of your sight. While I was over there, you remembered there was a book upstairs you wanted to add to the group. That gave me the opportunity to look over all the signed photos of important people you and Howard had up in your entrance hall."

Now Tanya's brow wrinkled. This was it, I could tell. That moment from earlier today when I knew something, but didn't know what it was, was when Tanya had gotten worried.

"While I was looking at the photos, I kept finding myself returning to one particular photo," I said.

Tanya shrugged. "There are plenty of interesting pictures. Why wouldn't you find one of them appealing?"

"Yes, but this isn't one of the ones you'd *think* I'd keep returning to. It wasn't a photo of you and Howard with a president or a celebrity. It was a photo of a climber."

Tanya gave a short laugh. "If you knew much about the world of climbing, you'd realize these climbers *are* celebrities. Especially the solo climbers, who scale mountains without the aid of ropes. They perform remarkable feats. Their progress up the mountains represent some of the highest forms of human achievement. They are featured in films and on the covers of magazines like *National Geographic.*"

"They have book deals?" I asked archly.

Tanya took in a hissing breath.

"Apparently, they do," I said. "Because Luna and I saw one of the books when we were in the basement after Carmen fell. Which, to me, is evidence you were down there, too."

Tanya's eyes were worried, but she said, "As if that's any real evidence."

"Oh, I think the police would find it very interesting you were down there when you'd claimed not to be at the library that day. The signed book definitely hadn't been there be-fore—Luna commented on it herself and said she'd like to buy the book when it went on sale. She also mentioned it was signed to a board member. What possible reason could you have to lie about something like that, otherwise?"

Tanya said, "You really don't understand *anything*, do you? There are plenty of reasons to lie, all the time. I have an impor-tant position in this town."

"And you didn't want any scandal to interfere with that po-sition, did you?" I asked.

Tanya said, "It's not just that. I don't want my mom to hear about any scandal. She doesn't deserve it." Her voice had risen sharply. "She's always been so proud of our family name and our place in Whitby. In her final years, she doesn't need to worry about prurient whispers and gossip."

"Which is exactly why you had to kill Howard. He knew you'd murdered Carmen. He wasn't a stupid man. And you needed to silence him before he went to the police," I said.

"The same way I need to silence you," hissed Tanya. "Didn't you think you were so smart? But intelligence doesn't always pay off."

She took a threatening step forward with the hammer, but I was ready for her. I reached out and grabbed the hardest, most punishing thing within arm's length: the library's copy of *Ulysses*. As Tanya swung at me, I swung at her. For all Tanya's de-termination, I was a lot younger than she was. And pretty deter-mined, myself, to stay alive.

Tanya gave a grunting gasp as the hammer was knocked out of her hand. She grabbled for it on my hardwood floor and I took the opportunity to hit her again as hard as I could on the back of the head with the heavy book.

She was out like a light. With shaking hands, I took my cell phone out of my pocket and called Burton.

# Chapter Twenty-Two

Burton was there within minutes, along with an ambulance. He took just a few moments to grimly survey the scene in front of him and briefly speak with me before gesturing to the paramedic and EMT to examine Tanya. Then he spoke with Tanya while she was sitting in the ambulance. Finally, he came over to speak with me.

"Has she confessed?" I asked anxiously.

Burton smiled at me. "She was reluctant to, at first. But she changed her mind when I turned on the voice recorder you handed me."

I smiled back at him.

"Could you fill me in a little more as to what exactly happened?" he asked.

I took a deep breath. "Tanya followed me tonight, although I was too tired and lost in my thoughts to really realize it. She was in the library parking lot when I left—I thought she was a patron who was taking forever to leave when I was trying to close up."

"And she followed you home?"

"That's right. I didn't even realize she was behind me until she said something. She'd apparently picked up on the fact that I knew something that might point to her."

Burton asked, "So she was threatening right away?"

"No, but she was off. That's why I turned on the voice recorder. She made up an excuse about exercising as to why she was there. But she forced me inside the house with that hammer," I said.

Burton's face was grim. "Yeah, that hammer was one of Blake's missing pieces of equipment. It's even got his initials on the base."

I stared at him. "Tanya intended for Blake to get the blame? But that doesn't make sense. She and Howard thought of Blake as their own son."

Burton said in a tired voice, "I guess that must have been true for a while, but when push came to shove, Tanya wanted to save herself. Her main instinct was for self-preservation. She sent the email implicating him, too. Apparently, she was very concerned about her mother finding out Tanya had murdered Carmen and Howard."

I nodded. "She'd mentioned before that she wants to protect her mother from anything that might upset her. Apparently, she thought I knew something and she was determined to silence me for good."

Burton quirked an eyebrow. "Clearly, you *did* know something."

"Yes, but I didn't really know what it was I knew and I didn't have much time to think about it, either. The library has been completely crazy. But when I was at Tanya's house earlier, waiting for her to gather books together, I was looking at a bunch of their photos," I said.

Burton frowned. "What, you were leafing through her photo albums?"

"No, these were on the wall. Tanya and Howard have apparently always loved entertaining, especially when their guests are important people of some kind. They have signed photos from movie stars and politicians. And athletes. They'd host them at a dinner and they'd sign the photos."

Burton's frown deepened and he looked even more confused.

"One of those photos was of a free solo climber. You know—those guys that scale some of the toughest mountains in the world without any ropes or harnesses or anything."

Burton said slowly, "So . . . crazy people."

"Maybe. Anyway, it reminded me of something I couldn't immediately put my finger on. But later, when Tanya was confronting me, I remembered what it was. After finding Carmen at the bottom of the stairs, there was a particular book from the book sale that sort of stood out—it was an autographed copy of one of the free solo guy's books," I said. "It was lying on the basement steps."

Burton rubbed his forehead as if it was hurting. "Okay, so that clearly points to Tanya being involved in the book sale."

"Exactly. Who else would have a signed copy of that particular book in a town like Whitby?"

Burton said, "But we know she was always there for library business. That she's even on the library board."

"Yes, but that book wasn't with the other books for the library sale," I said. "Plus, Luna mentioned *she'd* like to buy the book. That it hadn't been there before."

"You're saying it was dropped by the killer," said Burton, nodding slowly.

"Or maybe just put down when she was checking to see if Carmen was all right. Then she completely forgot about it when she realized Carmen was dead. What's more, we all thought Tanya hadn't even shown up for helping Carmen, which is why I got drafted by Wilson. And that was really out of the ordinary. When Tanya said she was going to show up at the library, she showed up. Sure enough, she'd been there that morning. But she left as soon as she realized what she'd done."

Burton sighed. "And it was all about an affair."

"An affair, for sure. But maybe also about her station in this town and how everyone viewed her as an important figure. As something of a leader, herself. Tanya was involved in everything, after all. She was very influential since she knew everyone and was married to the mayor. She came from an old family and old money and she cared a lot about protecting her mother. The last thing she wanted was any kind of a scandal," I said.

Burton said, "Why not just tell them both to knock it off? Why go to the bother of killing them?"

I said, "I'm guessing Carmen's death was a result of Tanya just lashing out at her. Tanya must have been furious. She's always wanted to be in control and Carmen was the same way. They butted heads all the time. Maybe Carmen said something snide to Tanya—Carmen could sometimes be that way. Tanya doesn't seem like the kind of person who would put up with that. It could have been planned, but I'm thinking most likely it was just an argument that got out of hand."

Burton nodded. "Tanya said her husband guessed she'd been responsible. Apparently, he'd been suspicious since Carmen's death—mostly because of the circumstances. It happened at the library and Tanya was at the library. Or, at least, he knew that's where she'd *planned* on being. But when Tanya returned home, she told him she *hadn't* been at the library."

"That would have been really unusual behavior for Tanya. She was one of those people who always showed up for everything she was supposed to do. And was there early, too. That must have been a real red flag for Howard. Then he'd have found out about Carmen's death and put two and two together," I said.

"Exactly. Tanya said that's exactly what he did do. He wasn't one to avoid confrontation, either, so he asked her about it directly. When she didn't answer him immediately, Howard knew. He told her she needed to go directly to the police and tell them what had happened. That she should only get manslaughter. Howard told her she wouldn't be able to live with herself otherwise and *he* wouldn't be able to live with her, either."

I winced. "Which was precisely what Tanya didn't want. The last thing she wanted was for her mother to find out what Tanya had done. She wanted absolutely no shame for the family. To her, the only way to stop her mother from finding out was by silencing Howard for good."

Burton said, "Right. But she should have known she'd have to *keep* killing to cover up what she'd done. That she'd keep being wary and suspicious that people knew what she'd done—like you."

I shivered and Burton continued briskly, "Let's change the subject. By the way," said Burton, coloring a little, "I finally talked with Luna about the study buddies event, like you said."

"How did that go?" I asked. Luna hadn't even mentioned it to me, which meant she saw it strictly in the realm of Library Business and not something personal.

Burton gave me a grin. It broke my heart a little to see him look so pleased. "It was good! She thought collaborating with the police department was a solid idea so we went right to Wilson with it. And he immediately signed off on it. Looks like it'll be on the calendar in the next few months."

"Great! I'll be sure to mention it to teens and moms at the circulation desk. Maybe we can get Fitz to advertise it on social media, too. He's good for attendance," I said.

"Maybe he can make a special appearance at the event?" asked Burton.

"I'm sure he'd love it. He's always lounging in the Young Adult nook and the kids seem to love him."

"That sounds perfect," said Burton, a happy lilt in his voice. "Now you need to turn in. It must have been a very long day for you today."

"It was long even before this happened," I admitted in a rueful voice.

Burton shook his head and laughed. "And to think heavy literature came to your rescue."

I smiled back at him. "Now I'm eternally grateful to *Ulysses*. The only reason the book was there was because I hadn't finished reading it. I suppose that means I'm going to have to finish it now. Suddenly, I feel a lot more motivated to."

"Ann? Ann? Are you okay? What's going on?"

I turned and saw Grayson hurrying up from the street.

Burton chuckled and said, "Looks like you're not going to get cracking on *Ulysses* tonight after all."

"Oh, Grayson and I are just friends. Barely even that," I stammered.

"Really? Doesn't look that way to me," said Burton as he winked at me and walked away, whistling as Grayson strode toward me.

# About the Author:

Elizabeth writes the Southern Quilting mysteries and Memphis Barbeque mysteries for Penguin Random House and the Myrtle Clover series for Midnight Ink and independently. She blogs at ElizabethSpannCraig.com/blog, named by Writer's Digest as one of the 101 Best Websites for Writers. Elizabeth makes her home in Matthews, North Carolina, with her husband. She's the mother of two.

Sign up for Elizabeth's free newsletter to stay updated on releases:

https://elizabethspanncraig.com/newsletter/

# This and That

I love hearing from my readers. You can find me on Facebook as Elizabeth Spann Craig Author, on Twitter as elizabethscraig, on my website at elizabethspanncraig.com, and by email at elizabethspanncraig@gmail.com.

Thanks so much for reading my book...I appreciate it. If you enjoyed the story, would you please leave a short review on the site where you purchased it? Just a few words would be great. Not only do I feel encouraged reading them, but they also help other readers discover my books. Thank you!

Did you know my books are available in print and ebook formats? And most of the Myrtle Clover series is available in audio. Find them on Audible or iTunes.

Interested in having a character named after you? In a preview of my books before they're released? Or even just your name listed in the acknowledgments of a future book? Visit my Patreon page at https://www.patreon.com/elizabethspanncraig .

I have Myrtle Clover tote bags, charms, magnets, and other goodies at my Café Press shop: https://www.cafepress.com/ cozymystery

If you'd like an autographed book for yourself or a friend, please visit my Etsy page.

I'd also like to thank some folks who helped me put this book together. Thanks to my cover designer, Karri Klawiter, for her awesome covers. Thanks to my editors, Zoe Nightingale and Judy Beatty, for all of their help. Thanks to beta readers Amanda Arrieta and Dan Harris for all of their helpful suggestions and careful reading. Thanks, as always, to my family and readers.

# Other Works by the Author:

Myrtle Clover Series in Order (be sure to look for the Myrtle series in audio, ebook, and print):

Pretty is as Pretty Dies

Progressive Dinner Deadly

A Dyeing Shame

A Body in the Backyard

Death at a Drop-In

A Body at Book Club

Death Pays a Visit

A Body at Bunco

Murder on Opening Night

Cruising for Murder

Cooking is Murder

A Body in the Trunk

Cleaning is Murder

Edit to Death

Hushed Up

A Body in the Attic (2020)

**Southern Quilting Mysteries in Order:**

Quilt or Innocence

Knot What it Seams
Quilt Trip
Shear Trouble
Tying the Knot
Patch of Trouble
Fall to Pieces
Rest in Pieces
On Pins and Needles
Fit to be Tied
Embroidering the Truth (2020)
**The Village Library Mysteries in Order:**
Checked Out
Overdue
Borrowed Time (2020)
**Memphis Barbeque Mysteries in Order (Written as Riley Adams):**
Delicious and Suspicious
Finger Lickin' Dead
Hickory Smoked Homicide
Rubbed Out
**And a standalone "cozy zombie" novel:** Race to Refuge, written as Liz Craig

Made in the USA
Monee, IL
18 September 2024

66130540R00125